REUNITED

Rosie followed him, eager to vacate the premises.

He stopped short, causing her to stumble over the rug. She fell forward, but he caught her. His hand slid around her waist, and he was careful not to topple over with her.

She was off balance and grabbed hold of his arms to right herself. "LeMar, what are you . . ." His lips pressed gently against hers before she could finish her sentence. The urge to return his kiss and revel in his embrace was so strong that she had to fight with herself to push him away.

BOOK YOUR PLACE ON OUR WEBSITE AND MAKE THE ARABESQUE ROMANCE CONNECTION!

We've created a customized website just for our very special Arabesque readers, where you can get the inside scoop on everything that's going on with Arabesque romance novels.

When you come online, you'll have the exciting opportunity to:

- View covers of upcoming books

- Learn about our future publishing schedule (listed by publication month and author)

- Find out when your favorite authors will be visiting a city near you

- Search for and order backlist books

- Check out author bios and background information

- Send e-mail to your favorite authors

- Join us in weekly chats with authors, readers and other guests

- Get writing guidelines

- AND MUCH MORE!

Visit our website at
http://www.arabesquebooks.com

REUNITED

Bridget Anderson

BET Publications, LLC
www.bet.com
www.arabesquebooks.com

ARABESQUE BOOKS are published by

BET Publications, LLC
c/o BET BOOKS
One BET Plaza
1900 W Place NE
Washington, DC 20018-1211

All Kensington Titles, Imprints, and Distributed Lines are available at special quantity discounts for bulk purchases for sales promotions, premiums, fund-raising, and educational or institutional use. Special book excerpts or customized printings can also be created to fit specific needs. For details, write or phone the office of the Kensington special sales manager: Kensington Publishing Corp., 850 Third Avenue, New York, NY 10022, attn: Special Sales Department, Phone: 1-800-221-2647.

First Printing: September 2001
10 9 8 7 6 5 4 3 2 1

Printed in the United States of America

This one is dedicated to everyone who encourages me to keep at it. To those of you who keep asking, "When's that next book coming out?" And to everyone who's ever written to me to let me know just how much you enjoy my work.

Well, it took me over a year, but here's to you.

One

"They've done what?!" Rosie Wright weaved through the mall's crowd, dodging bodies as she talked on her cellular phone to her sister, Doreece.

"Sold it. I'm looking at big black letters plastered across a Century 21 sign: SOLD."

"Don't tell me that. I didn't know it was up for sale. How could that house have sold so fast without even going on the market?" Rosie made her way out to the parking lot.

"Easy. Somebody came up with some money."

"You know what I mean. When I stopped by that house, they never mentioned anything to me about wanting to sell. It needs a lot of work." She unlocked the door to her black Acura Legend and climbed inside.

"Now what are you going to do?" Doreece asked.

"I don't know yet." Rosie picked at her nail polish. "Man, this ruins all my plans. I wanted that house."

"You should have asked them if they wanted to sell, then made an offer."

"Yeah, right. With what? They don't take Monopoly money. Or have you got some stashed away you could have loaned me?"

Doreece laughed. "Get real. You almost made me

run into a parked car. If I had a large sum of money, do you think I'd still be living in an apartment?"

"Well, it doesn't matter. Unless business picks up, the only place I'll be moving to is back into my basement. I did want that house—but it was out of my price range anyway."

"Don't sound so depressed. Things are going to pick up. You put me on the payroll part-time to help with marketing, remember? As a matter of fact, I'm on my way to pick up the new brochures you ordered now."

Rosie pulled out of the parking lot into traffic. "Oh, boy, I'd almost forgotten about those brochures. I need them for the Colony House." How could she afford Doreece? Business had to get better soon or she'd have to help Doreece find another job.

"Okay, we all have our objectives for the third quarter. Before you head back to your desks and start making the most of your day, I'd like to introduce the newest member of our team." Tom Fitzgerald, VP of the Southern Region, turned to the man on his left.

LeMar Reed smiled jauntily when all eyes focused on him. He'd already met most of his peers earlier when his boss had introduced him around. His boss had walked him around for everybody to get a look at the new kid on the block.

"LeMar Reed is our new Southeastern manager, for those of you who haven't met him yet. He comes to us from Washington, D.C., with a wealth of knowledge in the information management field. I'm sure he's going to be a great asset to this team—LeMar." Tom turned the floor over to him.

LeMar thanked his boss before clearing his throat.

"I'm looking forward to working with all of you as much as I'm looking forward to living in Atlanta again. I attended school here twelve years ago, so it's like coming home. I'm sure this is going to be a win-win move for me and Skynet," he said. "Thank you for welcoming me into the group."

On the way back to his office he noticed that the demographics of the Atlanta office were different from D.C.'s. There appeared to be an equal number of women to men, but, unexpectedly, there were far more sisters than brothers. Grace stopped him in the hallway. She was an attractive woman with long blond hair and sizable blue eyes. He guessed she was around thirty years old. She'd sat across the table from him in the meeting trying not to make eye contact.

"LeMar, I just wanted to say welcome again." Grace held out her hand to him.

"Thank you. I appreciate that." LeMar shook her hand.

"You said you went to school here. Where did you go?"

"Clark Atlanta." He began sizing Grace up as they walked slowly down the corridor.

"A Clark man, huh?" She smiled at him.

"For two years, then I transferred to Howard University. Maybe I'm half Clark and half Howard," he replied with a grin. When they reached his office door, he glanced around and caught a few stares as Grace talked nonstop. What was her story?

"Well, if I can do anything to help you out around here, let me know." With a flirtatious smile, she lightly touched his shoulder. "I know most of the people on this floor, and I've got a few buddies upstairs. Let's do lunch sometime."

"Sure, thanks a lot." He walked into his office. His

first day on the job, and he already had a lunch invitation. He looked at his phone, expecting to have
a few messages, but the message-waiting light was not
lit. He unpacked a few boxes while he waited for a
call from his Realtor.

Midway through his unpacking, the phone rang.
He answered, glad to hear his old school friend Eddie on the other end.

"Hey, man, what's up?" LeMar asked, moving to
his chair.

"Nothing much, baby boy. How's the new job?"

"It's cool. I think I'm going to like it here."

"Yeah. How many sisters working up there? I know
the place is crawling with them."

LeMar laughed. "Man, you're always looking for
another woman. What's up, you free and single
again?"

"As a bird. And ready to test my new wings. What
you got up for tonight?"

"Not a thing. I'll be pacing around that little ass
apartment until my Realtor calls."

"Meet me at Café Echelon tonight. We've got to
have a drink and celebrate your return to Hotlanta.
Man, you're not going to believe how much this place
has changed."

LeMar hoped a few things hadn't changed, or on
person in particular. "Give me a time and I'll b
there."

LeMar leaned against the bar, sipping from hi
glass of Hennessy. Eddie was wrong about one thing
Not much had changed about Atlanta's nightlife in
twelve years. New clubs, but the same scene. The
women still wore their dresses up to their thighs, and
when they bent over, the sun shined. He couldn't

believe the play he was getting tonight. If he didn't have another woman on his mind, it would have been great. Even Eddie had women checking him out.

"Hey, man, stop holding up the bar." Eddie approached LeMar from behind with a drink in his hand and a smile that spelled trouble.

LeMar gave him a sharp look. Fast Eddie was his nickname in college. He could talk anybody into just about anything. LeMar always thought he'd be the world's greatest salesman. His short, stocky build may not have attracted women, but his silver tongue always managed to do the trick.

"What you up to?" LeMar observed that Eddie hadn't changed much. He still absently stroked his mustache when he spotted a woman he wanted to meet.

Eddie shook his head. "Just checking out the ladies tonight." He leaned closer and yelled over the music. "Man, what do you think of this place? The women are fly, aren't they?"

LeMar took another sip from his drink. "There's some lookers in here," he answered, glancing around the room.

"Huh, more than that. I see a couple of freaks I'd like to have tonight."

LeMar laughed at the crude remark. "I see you're still chasing all the women?"

"Chasing and catching them, my man." He reached out to a woman passing by. "Hey, baby, what's your name?"

The woman ignored him and wiped the spot he'd touched.

LeMar snickered and turned around to face the bar. "Eddie, I think you need a new rap."

Eddie sat down next to him. "Nah, in a minute

she'll be looking for me. But I might not want her then."

Ignoring him, LeMar ordered another drink. "So, what have you been up to?"

Staring into his drink, Eddie answered, "Just trying to survive. Doing a little of this and that, whatever I can get."

"So where you working now?"

"I'm not."

"What happened?"

"Man, a brother can't get a break in this town. I've been looking for work for months now. I'm about to give up."

"You can't find work in Atlanta? I thought you said the job market here was good?" He knew Eddie had a tendency to stretch the truth.

"That's what everybody thinks, until they get here. Shoot, too many people are working damn minimum-wage jobs, and I ain't going out like that. I may not have finished college, but I got through two years in that mother."

"Why didn't you tell me before we came here?"

"Don't worry about it, brother. You're taking care of the drinks tonight." He patted LeMar's back and motioned for the bartender. "Hey, my man, hit me one more time."

Laughing, LeMar set his empty glass on the counter. That was Eddie's third drink. "Same old Eddie."

"You know I ain't ever going to change." He turned his gaze to follow a woman in a micromini dress across the room.

LeMar followed his gaze and noticed the woman. "She reminds me of Christine. Remember her?"

"Hell, you should see her now. She's gained about two hundred pounds. But boy, back in the day—"

Both of them laughed and began their journey down memory lane. They spent the next hour discussing old college friends. LeMar had only returned to Atlanta once, for his job interview, since he'd transferred to Howard University twelve years ago.

"Man, you'd be surprised how many people stayed right here in Atlanta after school. Give yourself a couple of weeks, you'll start seeing people."

LeMar looked straight ahead into the mirror behind the bar. He had a good view of the room. The crowd had picked up, and the night reminded him of his college days.

"Eddie, do you remember when we talked a couple of months ago?"

"Yeah, about you relocating."

"You said you ran into Rosie one day, didn't you?"

Eddie shook his head for a few seconds without saying anything, then he smiled. "Man, you still thinking about her, aren't you?"

LeMar didn't lie. "Sometimes. She still lives here, doesn't she?"

"That was a couple of years ago, but I reckon so."

"Is she still married?"

"I don't think so. It was kind of early so we didn't exactly chitchat, you know. She looked good, I looked good, what more do you need to know?"

"It was before you went to work, huh?" LeMar laughed, changing the subject.

Eddie slammed his drink on the table. "Damn you, man." He elbowed LeMar playfully. "Everybody ain't got it going on like you. Come on, let's get out of here." He pulled a few dollars out of his pocket and threw them on the bar.

LeMar shoved the money back at him and laughed, knowing it was all for show. "You're making me pay tonight, remember?"

Quickly, Eddie grabbed his money and shoved it back into his pocket. "That's right. You're the man with all the Benjamins."

LeMar ignored him and followed him outside. He hadn't wanted to discuss Rosie with Eddie. He just needed a little information from him.

"Hey, think you can drop me off?" Eddie asked. "My car's in the shop right now."

"Sure. It's no problem." He probably didn't have a car. They left the club, and LeMar followed Eddie's directions through downtown. He thought about Rosie and wondered how she was doing. To him, she would always be the one who got away. She was the subconscious reason he'd accepted the transfer.

"You can drop me off on the corner up there." Eddie pointed out the window to a corner store.

"I can take you all the way home, no problem."

"That's okay, I need to see this buddy of mine before I go home."

"Sure." LeMar pulled his Land Rover over to the curve, dodging debris and broken bottles. He let his friend out. He didn't worry about Eddie. Eddie had a way of blending in with whatever crowd there was.

On his way home, LeMar rode past the Varsity, a popular downtown hamburger joint and college hangout. He remembered how Rosie loved their fries and shakes and the antics of the waiters on roller skates. They used to sit in the car and eat and talk for hours.

Rosie walked into Sylvia's, a soul food restaurant in the heart of downtown Atlanta, fifteen minutes late for her business lunch. She gave the host her name and looked around as he escorted her to a small table in the back. Nathan Williams stood as she approached the table.

Rosie held out her hand. "Hello, Mr. Williams, sorry I'm late. Downtown traffic is crazy." An uncomfortable shiver ran down her spine as they stood almost toe-to-toe. She guessed that, in her heels, she was about an inch or two taller than he was.

He shook her hand and pulled out her chair. Simultaneously, he checked her out from head to toe. "Please, call me Nathan. It's no problem. I just arrived myself." He sat back down and smiled.

Rosie returned the smile and tried not to focus on his receding hairline and shiny forehead. He had the largest black-owned furniture store in Atlanta, and she needed his help. When they'd met several months ago at a networking event, she'd told him about her design business. He was interested, but in more than her work. She hadn't encouraged him then, nor would she today.

"I like that suit. You know, you're looking fine as usual."

"Thank you." She glanced at him, then back down at her menu. "Have you ordered yet?"

"No. Our waiter should be here any minute now." He looked around the restaurant.

"Nathan, thanks for this opportunity to talk with you about my volunteer work. When I tell most business owners I design and decorate a house for the poor every year, they aren't interested in donating anything. I'm glad you can see this as something positive for the community, as well as your company."

"Your proposal did interest me. From what I understand, you need a different sponsor to help furnish each room. And you want them to donate all of the furniture, right?" he inquired.

"Well, I'm going for two sponsors for the entire

house. One for the major furniture and appliances, and one financial sponsor. I'll shop yard sales and discount stores to complete the house. You'd be amazed at how many rooms I can furnish for as little as five thousand dollars."

"The whole house?" he asked with a puzzled look. "That hardly seems possible."

"Not counting any major appliances, it is. You have to remember, these are starter homes, so they're not very large."

"So you'd like five thousand dollars for this project, in addition to the furniture from my store?"

Rosie raised her chin and looked him square in the eye. "Correct. Nathan, the donated furniture is a tax write-off, and you'll get great publicity for donating to the Colony House. Colony Homes Builders donate a free home every year, and I decorate it for them. It'll be advertised on the radio."

Nathan shook his head as he tapped his fingers against the table. "Oh, I'm not disputing it's for a good cause. I am interested in sponsorship in some way. You know, I'm always looking to help my people whenever I can. However, I'll have to think about this."

Rosie hoped he wasn't about to change his mind. She couldn't let him back out; she needed his money. Her heart raced as she turned up the pressure. "I can understand your hesitation—"

The minute he made himself comfortable by resting his elbow on the table, the waiter appeared. They placed their lunch order.

Rosie continued before she lost him. "Nathan, the reason I'm asking you to donate both is because people in the community know your company's name. Williams Furnishings has a great reputation for treating people right. When folks hear you're outfitting the house, they'll want to do business with you even more."

"What makes you think that?" He looked at her sharply.

"Because I know the black community. I've been in a lot of homes and talked with a lot of people. They like companies that give back to the community they do business in."

"We do that."

Now it's time to stroke that ego. "I know you do, and I've got confidence that this project will appeal to you and become your annual project as well."

He smiled and slowly ran his tongue across his bottom lip. "Well, I'll have to go over this with my partners, but I think we could have a good time working together."

She stared at him, then noticed the waiter approaching with their lunch. "We wouldn't be working together on a daily basis or anything. However, you'd definitely benefit from all the marketing."

He shook his head and placed his napkin in his lap. "So what does your husband think of this project?"

"I'm not married. However, if I were, he'd think it was a great idea," she affirmed.

"I don't know. If I had a woman as fine as you at home, I'd be a little jealous."

"Of what?" she asked with raised brows. She hoped he wasn't about to go down the wrong lane with her.

"Somebody stealing you from me. For example, a man like myself, who finds you incredibly sexy." His voice took on a low, husky tone.

Rosie dropped her fork. No, he didn't! "Nathan—I think we should keep things on a professional level. Let's not mix business with pleasure. I'm flattered, but I keep my personal life separate from my business."

"My business is my pleasure. This is a business lunch, and I find it very pleasurable." He took a bite of his steak and chewed while staring at her.

"As much as I enjoy my job, I'd like for us to work on a professional level." Finally she added, "It's my business policy." She wasn't interested in him, and she wanted him to know it.

He cocked his head to the side and grinned at her. "I see. I suppose you couldn't be persuaded to change your mind, either?"

Her eyes grew wider with astonishment. "No, and I don't plan to start. Sorry." She shrugged.

He held up his hands. "Okay, I can take a hint. Conflict of interest and all. But after this project of yours is over"—he leaned across the table—"I'm coming to get you, lady." He leaned back in his seat, observing her response with a cocky smile on his face.

Rosie bit the inside of her cheek to keep from laughing aloud. *I should be so lucky.* She forced the corners of her mouth up into a smile and pictured herself as the Joker from the *Batman* movie. If she gave him a hint of the disgusting snarl she wanted to display, he'd never help her.

"So does that mean you've already decided to invest in my project?"

"I'm considering it more and more every minute. However, if I chose not to, we won't be business associates. Then you're free to date me, right?"

"Actually, no. I'd be too upset to go out with you. After all, I'd hoped to convince you to write me a check this afternoon."

Nate laughed. "You're smooth. I like that in a woman."

"Not half as smooth as you." She gave him her sexiest grin. "So what do you say?" She couldn't risk him backing out now.

"I'll tell you what." He rested his elbows on the table. "I'm going to a benefit dance this weekend, and I might be able to make that decision a little faster with you on my arm."

"Excuse me?" She blinked several times. "You'll have to repeat that because I know I didn't hear you right."

"I invited you to a dance this weekend, nothing more."

"And if I go it'll help you make up your mind?" She scrunched up her nose.

"It might be worth five thousand dollars to me. That is, if we have a good night."

Oh, no, he didn't!

Two

Rosie met Sharon at Mick's in Buckhead for lunch. Ever since they'd first met five years ago in design school, they got together a couple of times a month to gossip and discuss their problems.

"You mean that little dweeb put the moves on you? I can't believe it. He struts around town like he's such a righteous brother." Sharon took the last piece of bread as she listened to Rosie give details of her lunch with Nathan.

"Girl, he turned a simple business lunch into a proposition. I'm surprised he didn't come out and ask me for sex in exchange for the money."

"Sounds like he did, in so many words. You know what he meant by, 'if the night goes well,'" she mocked Nathan. "He's looking to get in those panties," she said, laughing.

"Yeah, well, he can hold his breath until that happens." Rosie rolled her eyes. "I was so insulted. I don't know what made him think he could approach me like that. I presented myself in a very professional manner. Besides, his business gets plenty of publicity in exchange for his sponsorship."

"I hope you told him to get lost." Sharon pushed her plate away and looked around for the waiter.

When Rosie didn't respond, Sharon glanced back at her.

"You did blow him off, right?"

Rosie hesitated. "Not quite."

"Rosie! What were you thinking about?"

"Money. It's not like sponsors are knocking down my door to help me here. And the ones from last year aren't coming back. That family will move into an empty house if I don't get enough sponsorship to complete the work. Girl, I do not need any bad publicity."

"So he's going to give you the money, hoping one day you'll go out with him?"

"Something like that. I told him I had plans for Saturday night so I don't have to go to that dance with him."

Sharon's eyes narrowed with suspicion. "You aren't really going anywhere with him, are you?"

"Of course not. You know me better than that. I'll be busy until after the house is complete."

"Well, make sure you are. If you tell me you went out with that man, I'm going to give you a real hard time."

The waiter took their empty plates and left the bill.

"Don't worry. I'm not that hard up for a date." Rosie chuckled.

"Speaking of . . ." Sharon put her money on the table, then pulled a piece of paper out of her purse. "Are you going to the African Grapevine's dance next month?"

"Whose?" Rosie reached for the paper.

"You remember that networking group I told you about. I joined a couple of months ago. I'm sure there'll be a lot of single men there."

Rosie read the flyer about the soiree being held at a local nightclub. "Think I can meet some clients through this group?"

"Sure you can. It's all about networking. It's also a great way to meet men. Besides, you need to get out more. I can't seem to get you to do anything these days. You're always working."

"Sharon, that's how it is when you have your own business."

"Yeah, that's what you say, but I think it's your way of avoiding men."

"What?" Rosie asked, laughing. "Why would I do that?"

"You're scared to get into another relationship for some reason. Since your divorce I've watched you chase away some very eligible men. Men I can't seem to meet."

"I haven't chased anybody away. Like I said, I don't have time to date right now."

"Girl, you make time for a man, you hear me? I don't care how busy you are." Sharon glanced at her watch. "Speaking of busy, I hate to run off so fast, but I've got to get back. Things are crazy at work. You know how it is."

"Sure. I need to get going myself. I've got tons of calls to make this afternoon."

"You did say you were looking for more sponsors, right?" Sharon asked.

"I sure am. Do you know somebody who could make a financial donation? It's tax deductible." The women gathered their purses and headed for the exit.

"I just might. I'll talk with my boss. He's always giving money to charity."

"Thanks, Sharon. I appreciate that," Rosie said, weaving through the lunch crowd gathered at the entrance.

"That's what friends are for."

* * *

Grace, LeMar, and Todd, a manager at Skynet, pulled into Mick's parking lot for lunch. LeMar glanced around the area. Twelve years ago, he hadn't frequented the Buckhead area much.

Todd pulled up to the front door. "I'll let you guys out here while I park next door."

They got out of the car at the restaurant entrance.

LeMar opened the restaurant door for Grace. Before she could step in, Rosie walked out. Surprised and shocked, LeMar could only stare at her.

Rosie looked up at him, then at Grace, then back at him. Her heartbeat sped up and she almost lost her breath. She was staring at the face she hadn't expected to see ever again.

"Rosie!" he said, letting her name hang in the air. His head filled with wonderful memories. Since returning to Atlanta, LeMar thought about her every day. Had the power of positive thinking summoned her?

Her light brown eyes checked him out from head to toe. He couldn't tell if she was happy or upset, but he was glad to finally lay eyes on her again.

"LeMar—hello. What are you doing in Atlanta?" Rosie couldn't believe her eyes. Her stomach turned somersaults, and the sight of him caused her body temperature to rise. She searched in her purse for her sunglasses as she moved out of the doorway.

"I live here now." He held the door, forgetting about Grace.

"Since when?" Rosie asked with her insides bubbling over. Here stood the one true love of her life, and the man who hurt her most.

"About a week ago. It's amazing running into you my first week in town. How have you been?" She looked stunning in her short skirt and jacket, which showed off her still-trim figure.

"I'm doing great, and you?"

"I'm okay." He shrugged and smiled. Suddenly, he felt like a college freshman meeting the woman of his dreams. He wanted to see that beautiful smile of hers.

"Looks like it." She looked inside the door at Grace, who had entered the restaurant and now stood by the hostess stand.

LeMar followed her gaze. "Oh, that's my coworker, Grace."

"Yeah, well, it was nice seeing you again." She wanted to walk away, but couldn't move. Her legs became lead pipes too heavy for her little body to move.

Sharon cleared her throat to grab Rosie's attention.

"You're not going to introduce me to this lovely lady?" LeMar couldn't let Rosie get away. He had so many questions. What had happened to them twelve years ago? How had they lost touch?

Rosie covered her mouth with her hand and turned to her best friend. "I'm sorry. Sharon, this is LeMar Reed, my . . ." She looked at LeMar, not sure how to introduce him.

He jumped in to let her off the hook. "We're old college friends." He smiled at Rosie. All he needed to see was her smile back at him.

She nodded and gave him the smile he'd been awaiting.

"Yes, we went to Clark Atlanta together years ago."

"It's nice to meet you, LeMar." Sharon offered her hand.

"It's a pleasure to meet you, too," he said, shaking her hand.

"Well, we've gotta be going. Enjoy your lunch." Rosie stepped away.

"Thank you, I will." As she walked away, LeMar checked her out from head to toe, noticing she still had a firm, lean body with nice legs. She looked even better than she had in college. He found himself wanting to sit down for lunch with her instead of his coworkers. He wanted to tell her all about his life since he'd seen her last and hopefully find out if she still had feelings for him.

Watching her get into her car, he wondered when he'd see her again. After twelve years their breakup still hurt, but that was okay; he was glad he'd seen her.

"Girl, don't tell me you let that man get away," Sharon said, getting into Rosie's car.

"I didn't *let* him do anything. Like he said, we're old friends." Rosie's heart still raced from the sight of him. He looked so toned and sexy. She'd momentarily lost her power of speech. He'd matured and looked even better than she remembered.

"So he wasn't your man?"

Rosie pulled out of the lot, trying to avoid Sharon's gaze. "Yeah, something like that."

Sharon nodded, contemplating what Rosie said. "That look expressed more than 'something like that' to me. He looked at you like he remembered a lot more than that."

Rosie banged her hand against the steering wheel. "Why did he have to move back here? I never wanted to see him again."

"Why not? He seems like a nice man."

"I just didn't." Rosie's tone was sharp and short. She hadn't told Sharon about LeMar, even though they were best friends.

"What's he? About six-two? And he looks like he's around two hundred solid masculine pounds. Damn, give him my number," Sharon suggested in a loud voice, rolling her eyes at Rosie.

Rosie couldn't help but laugh.

"I'm not joking. If he's over you, I'll go out with him." She crossed her arms.

"He's not trustworthy, but I've got a man for you."

"Who?"

"I'll introduce you to Nathan. He's looking for a good woman." Rosie shook her head and turned to Sharon before they burst into hysterics.

"Girl, I'm gonna hurt you." Sharon shook her finger at Rosie.

After Rosie dropped Sharon off, her thoughts raced back to LeMar. He was the only man she'd ever loved. Other than David, her ex-husband. However, her love for David had been different. He'd come into her life at a time when she'd needed someone. Pregnant and scared, her good friend David had comforted her and offered to marry her. Even after her miscarriage and the end of their marriage, they remained friends. LeMar was her first and only true love.

Rosie pulled up to Doreece's apartment building and dashed up two flights of stairs. Her persistent knocking revealed how anxious she was to talk about LeMar.

The door swung open. "What's the matter?" Doreece asked nervously.

"Nothing," Rosie said between breaths as she recovered from running up the stairs.

"Then why were you banging on the door like a crazy woman?" Doreece closed the door behind her. She walked across the small living room in a pair of black leggings and an oversize T-shirt.

"I wasn't banging, I knocked."

"Whatever." Doreece grabbed the television remote from her seat and lowered the volume.

"To what do I owe the honor of your presence so early in the day? Don't tell me you came by on my day off just to see me?"

"No, I came by to see if those carpet samples came in yesterday?"

Doreece tucked her foot beneath her and leaned back in the chair. "All you had to do was go into the office and you'd see they were there. Have you been in since lunch yesterday?"

"Of course I have. I didn't remember seeing the samples. I was in this part of town, so I thought—"

Doreece didn't let her finish. "Okay, who is he?"

"Who's who?" Rosie asked, surprised her sister knew her so well.

"The man who has you running by here pretending he doesn't exist."

Rosie leaned her head back on the couch and took a deep breath. Raising it again, she looked at Doreece. "I just saw LeMar at Mick's. He's moved back in town."

Doreece gave her a curious look. "Who's that?"

"My old boyfriend from college."

"The same LeMar who dumped you years ago and left you heartbroken?" she clarified.

"I wasn't heartbroken."

"Are we talking about the same man who caused you to drop out of college?"

Rosie jumped up. "Okay, I heard you. He wasn't the reason I left school, either." She paced around Doreece's living room with her hands on her hips, lying to herself.

"Sure he wasn't," Doreece replied, sarcastically.

"You know I still hate him for what he did to me. He smiled at me as if nothing ever happened."

"Man, he sure got under your skin. It doesn't sound like you've gotten over him yet."

Rosie stopped and stared at Doreece, flabbergasted. "Did you not hear what I said? I hate that man!" She flopped down onto the oversize love seat and threw her head back. *So, why did I get all excited at the sight of him?*

"What did he say to you?"

"Not much. He just moved back in town, and he had a lunch date already."

"If he still looks anything like the pictures you have, I'm surprised he's not married by now."

Rosie shrugged. "He might be. I don't know, and I don't care. Let's not discuss him. I don't want him to ruin my afternoon. I need to try and work on more sponsors today."

"Okay, so Mr. LeMar is old news. Let's change the subject."

Doreece hesitated a moment, then asked, "When's the last time you went out with a man anyway? And I don't mean any of those designer friends of yours. I mean a man who drives you crazy, like LeMar obviously does."

Rosie turned up her lip at Doreece. "You call that changing the subject?"

"Just answer the question."

"David was a real man."

"Oh, sure." Doreece crossed her arms. "To his girlfriend more than his wife. I think he liked being married. He got more women that way."

"Don't tell me about my husband. You only know what I told you. He was a friendly guy."

"Your ex-husband. I know what I saw, too. He was friendly all over town." Doreece waved her hand.

"But I'm not talking about him. You've only been out a couple of times since your divorce."

"I'm too busy. Plus, every man I meet wants advice on fixing up his house. I'm tired of exchanging decorating tips for dinners. Besides, I'm not a social butterfly like you. I like to keep my man count low."

A hurt expression crossed Doreece's face. She lowered her head and squinted at Rosie. "I didn't know I had a man count," she responded in an injured tone.

Rosie could have kicked herself. She'd offended her sister. "Doreece, I didn't mean anything by that. It's just that you always seem to have a date. You attract men even though you have a man. I'm too straitlaced and boring. I can count the men I've been out with on one hand."

"Yeah, I guess that's why I'm in the predicament I'm in now."

"What is it?" Rosie noticed Doreece's posture and demeanor change.

"I'm pregnant."

Three

Feeling completely satisfied LeMar clasped his hands behind his head and took a deep breath. He'd dreamed about home ownership for years. Now he could take advantage of the inexpensive real estate in Atlanta. Alone with his Realtor, Mary, he could talk more freely.

"Congratulations, Mr. Reed, you have yourself a beautiful home with great possibilities." Mary passed him an envelope.

"Thanks. I can't believe I walked off and left some papers behind after that closing."

"It's understandable. You're sure you've got everything, then you set something down. Everybody does it. I'm just glad I picked it up."

"Yeah, so am I. You know I can't wait to move out of that cramped apartment."

"Well, you have plenty of room now. I can't get over how lucky you were to get that house. That's the fastest sale I've ever made. I can't wait to see what you do with it. There are four huge bedrooms and three bathrooms. That's a lot of house for a single man. Planning on getting married anytime soon?"

"Not that I'm aware of," he said, laughing. "I guess I'd better start making some plans for my investment. I'm going to need a good decorator now."

* * *

After the movers left, LeMar sat down in front of the television in his den and stared at the phone. He reached for the phone book and flipped to the G's. His finger scrolled down the pages, searching for Greene. Richard, Ronald, Rosa, but no Rosie. He closed the phone book and shoved it across the table. What made him think she'd be listed under her maiden name? Maybe she was listed under her married name.

Besides, what would he say if he called her? Hello, would you like the chance to hurt me again? Stupidity could be the only thing that made him consider calling her.

The doorbell rang. LeMar went to see who'd found him already. Before he opened the front door, he could see Eddie through the beveled glass.

He swung the door open. "Welcome to the Reed Palace."

Eddie strolled in, shaking his head. "You mean the Reed Mansion." He looked around the foyer. "Where's the butler? Or even better, the maid."

"I haven't hired her yet." LeMar closed the door.

"Yeah, well, make sure she's young and pretty when you do."

"Come on in and check out my place."

"Man, this reminds me of the fraternity house you used to live in. You and those stuck-up friends of yours." Eddie snorted and turned up his nose. "And to think you almost talked me into pledging." He walked through the living room into the den, inspecting each room along the way.

LeMar followed him. "You should have."

"Are you kidding? No way I'm sharing a house with four other guys. Four other women, maybe. Besides, those boys didn't really know how to live. You gotta admit, you had a better time with me than those dudes."

Eddie sat on the edge of the soft leather couch, tapping his feet on the floor. The deep-seated, over-stuffed couch was more suited for LeMar's frame.

LeMar sat across from him in a matching chair. "Yeah, we did have some good times."

"Man, why did you buy this big house?"

"It's an investment. I might rent it out, I don't know."

"Hey, if you've got it going on like that. Like I said, you're the man with the Benjamins."

Eddie shifted in his seat. "Look, man, I hate to trouble you, but I need to ask a favor."

"Yeah, what's up?"

"You know I got your back if you need me, and I feel like I can count on you when I'm in a jam."

"Of course, man, what you need?" LeMar figured it wouldn't be long before Eddie wanted to borrow money. Just like in the old days.

"A place to stay for a couple of days. I know you just moved in and all, so if you say no, I understand."

"It's no problem. You can crash here. I remember that little fire at the frat house, and you let me camp out with you for a couple of weeks."

"Yeah, I did help you out, didn't I? Well, you know you're my boy. I'm always here for you."

"Same here. Now, tell me why you need a place to stay."

"Man, my woman's trippin'! She'll come to her senses in a few days. I need to make her miss me for a while. You know how it is." He rested his elbow on the arm of the couch.

"Yeah, I understand," he said, concluding that Eddie's girl kicked him out. "As long as you don't mind all the boxes and clutter, make yourself at home."

"Thanks, man. I won't be here long, a week or so at the most."

"Sure, no problem." LeMar reached over to the coffee table for the remote and flipped through the channels. "Hey, you won't believe this, but I ran into Rosie yesterday."

"Your girl Rosie?" Eddie asked, getting up.

"She's not my girl, but yeah, that Rosie."

"Got any beer?" Eddie left the den. "Where's the kitchen?" He called from the hallway.

"All the way back on the right," LeMar called out. "There are a few cans in there."

"You want one?"

"No, but help yourself." *As if he weren't going to,* LeMar thought.

When Eddie returned with his beer in hand, he stood in the doorway. "Where'd you see her at?"

"I went into Mick's with this white girl from work, and Rosie walked out right past us. I know she probably thought we were dating."

Eddie grinned. "You still trying to hit on that woman after all these years, huh?"

"Man, this is not about sex. What we had went deeper than a physical relationship. She still looks good, too."

"Is she still married?"

"I don't know. I didn't ask. We spoke, and she introduced me to a friend of hers. I didn't get her phone number or anything."

"You know, now that I think about it, I believe she is married." Eddie sat back down. "Yeah, I'm almost sure of it."

"Uh-huh." LeMar shook his head. "You're almost sure?"

"Yeah, but so what. Make your move. Throw some of that old-school charm on her. Women like that type of stuff. It makes them weak in the knees and ready."

LeMar laughed. "Not if she's married, man, and besides, it's not about sex."

"You're wrong, dude." He took another swig of his beer. "It's always about sex when it comes to women. You always were one of those romantic-type guys. But, man, I'm telling you, when it all boils down, everything's about sex."

LeMar wasn't surprised that Eddie felt that way. He'd never admitted to ever being in love, even at thirty-five. LeMar felt sorry for him.

"Meet the right woman, and you'll change your mind."

"I doubt it. I'm a realist. Love doesn't exist." Eddie spread his arms across the back of the couch. "So, whatever happened between you guys anyway?"

LeMar gave him a few details of their breakup twelve years ago. After he'd moved back to Maryland, he and Rosie had drifted apart. Later, he'd learned she'd gotten married. He knew Eddie didn't care, nor would he even understand how LeMar felt about her. However, if he knew the details, maybe he'd quit insisting sex would solve everything.

Rosie helped her assistant, Neville Broady, load paint and a few carpet samples into the back of his van. Lately, business had slacked off at Yahimba Designs, which shouldn't have been the case. As summer approached, business should have been picking up instead of declining.

"I'll take these over to the Browns this afternoon.

What are we working on next week?" Neville asked as he wiped his hands on an old towel.

She hated to deliver bad news. When Neville had started helping her a year ago, they couldn't keep up with all the business. Now, she wasn't even sure if she could keep him on.

Squinting from the sun, she glanced around. "I'm not sure. I don't have anything lined up for next week. Neville, I'm real sorry, business is kind of slow. I may need to cut your hours."

Neville took a deep breath. "I understand. I noticed things had slowed down. Does this mean I'm fired?"

"No, I'll still have some work for you. Trust me, things will turn around soon. Doreece is helping with marketing. It would help me out if you scaled back to three days a week for a little while. Just until things pick up again." She didn't want to lose him. He was an eager design student, and helped out tremendously.

"Sure, I guess it wouldn't kill me for a little while. I can concentrate on my studies more."

"Thanks, Neville. You're wonderful." She hugged him.

"Don't worry about it. I enjoy working for you. I'm learning more from you than I'm learning in most of my classes." He closed the van door and pulled out his keys.

"Neville, there's not much I can teach you. You have a great eye."

"Thanks. I'd better be running, I'm going to meet Roy. I'll see you on Friday night, right?"

"I'll be there." Rosie nodded.

"Good. Roy's looking forward to meeting you after hearing me talk about you so much."

"I hope it's all good," she said, walking away.

"Of course. What else could it be?"

* * *

Rosie rode down Interstate 285 wondering how she would be able to pay Doreece. She helped Rosie out three days a week, which was all Rosie could afford. She needed to get this project off the ground and completed in two months.

When she stepped through her office door, her sister met her.

"Guess what?" she asked, holding a calendar in her hand and smiling.

"What?"

"Oh, come on, guess."

"Doreece, I don't want to guess. What is it?" Rosie didn't need any surprises.

"You have an appointment tomorrow in midtown at 4322 Ponce de Leon."

"Isn't that the house I wanted?" Rosie took the calendar from her sister and read the next day's schedule.

"It sure is. A lady named Ms. Lurlay called to schedule a consultation. When she told me the address, I almost jumped out of my seat. Can you believe it?"

"No, I can't. How did she hear about us?"

"She didn't say. She said we came highly recommended, and she needed an initial consultation."

Rosie handed the calendar back, then walked over to her desk, opposite the small table Doreece used. "Isn't this weird? I didn't get to buy the house, but I might get to decorate it."

"Yeah, and that doesn't make you mad?" Doreece inquired.

"Not really. It's a beautiful house. Having the opportunity to work on it will be a pleasure. Plus, that house probably needs a lot of work." She winked. "Which means a lot of money."

"Well, you're excited about it, that's good."

"I get excited about all of my work. You know I love it. But it's not every day that you get to work on a house that old. Besides, I couldn't have afforded it anyway."

Doreece strolled back over to her table and began packing. "Well, I'm glad you're happy about it. In a way, you get your wish."

"Are you getting ready to leave?"

"Yeah, I'm going to see Tony." She grabbed her purse.

Rosie turned up her nose when she heard his name. "I—"

"Don't say it." Doreece held out her hand. "I know how you feel about him, and I don't want to hear it. I have something to say to him, and he's going to listen to me."

"Okay, if you want to put yourself through that, I can't stop you."

"You sure can't."

"But you don't have to chase him. Hasn't he done enough damage? For goodness' sake, he's not even man enough to admit he's the father."

"I know he's the father, and that's enough." Doreece stormed past Rosie toward the door.

"But is he ready to be a father?" Rosie stood, hoping to stop her little sister.

"I'm not going to let him walk out on me. This is his baby, and if I have to, I'll prove it to him." She marched out of the office and didn't look back.

Rosie sat down and shook her head. She'd seen that look on her own face. She prayed that her little sister could handle this.

* * *

Rosie pulled up to 4322 Ponce de Leon and stepped out of the car, smiling as she looked at the old house. The architecture was beautiful. She noticed the poorly kept yard as she approached the steps. She loved the huge front porch, and couldn't wait to transform this old house into a beautiful showcase.

She pressed the doorbell and waited for Ms. Lurlay to answer the door. Looking around at the light fixtures, she couldn't help but think about how much she'd wanted this to be her home. If only she'd had enough money for a down payment, she would have approached the former owners. The squeak of the front door caught her attention.

Rosie looked directly into LeMar's eyes. She stood there startled. A warm flush rushed to her face. Was this somebody's idea of a joke?

"Rosie!" He gave her a perplexed look.

"What are you doing here?" she asked, totally confused.

"I live here."

She looked down at her pad again. "I'm looking for Ms. Lurlay." *Maybe that was his wife. Why did she ask for me?*

"That's my secretary."

"Well . . ." Rosie checked her pad again. "Could this be some type of mix-up? I have an appointment with her at five-thirty. Or I'm supposed to." *God, I hope he doesn't think I was trying to find him.*

"You're with Yahimba Designs?"

She pointed at herself. "I am Yahimba Designs."

"You're kidding?" He smiled at Rosie.

"No, I'm not," she proudly exclaimed, resting a hand on her hip.

He stood back in the doorway, holding out his hand. "Please, come in. My secretary recommended your design firm, so I asked her to make the appointment. She should have put it in my name. I'm sorry."

Rosie hesitantly stepped inside the foyer. "This is your house?"

"Yes. I purchased it a week ago." He closed the door.

She suddenly became claustrophobic. He stood close enough for her to smell the robust scent of his cologne. This whole scene was too much for her. Standing face-to-face with him after all these years.

Rosie took a few steps and looked around the foyer as she experienced an overwhelming feeling of déjà vu. She'd been here with him before. Everything moved in slow motion. She began to perspire and fidget with her purse.

He tugged at the sleeve of his tan striped double-breasted suit. The tailored cut of the suit and the matching taupe silk jacquard tie gave him a sharp, pulled-together look. He looked cool and quite comfortable.

"This is unbelievable," Rosie said, after an awkward silence.

"What?"

She looked at him, not wanting to tell him about her interest in buying the house. "That your secretary called me of all people, not knowing that we knew each other." She shot him a suspicious glare.

LeMar held up his hands. "Hey, I promise you I had no idea she was calling you. She left me a note saying Neville would be by at five-thirty."

"Neville works with me," she said, averting her eyes. Now what to do? This was a mistake. She couldn't work on this house now, not with him here.

He slipped past her, sliding out of his jacket. "Let's

go into the den and talk. I just came in a few minutes before you rang the bell. I don't know exactly what I want. That's why I wanted to hire a designer."

She followed him down the hall into the den. *What am I doing? I've got to get out of here.* LeMar kept talking, however, and she didn't hear a word he said. She focused on the crown moldings, high ceilings, and details that gave the house character. The den appeared small with a couch, a few chairs, a television, and plenty of boxes.

"Well, what do you think?" he asked, motioning for her to have a seat.

"It's nice." She didn't really want to sit down, but she did. This situation caught her off guard. She tried to pull herself and her thoughts together.

"So, tell me about your company. How long have you been in business?"

She jumped up. "Look, LeMar, I don't think this is such a good idea. You didn't know I owned Yahimba Designs, so let's forget that I was ever here." She moved toward the door.

"Wait a minute." He followed her out of the den, trying to stop her. "Don't go."

She stopped and slowly turned to face him.

"I may not have known you owned the company, but that doesn't mean we can't work this out. I need my house decorated, and your company comes highly recommended."

"If I take this job, that means we'd see more of each other than I'm sure we'd like. Let's be realistic about this. We haven't seen each other in more than twelve years, and now you want me to decorate your house? I don't think so." She edged closer to the front door, her stomach quivering.

Things would never be right between them. She

wished he'd never come back to Atlanta. So much for her financial windfall.

LeMar followed her. "I know this feels a little awkward, but we're both adults. What happened years ago, we can't change. I'd like to think that we still have respect for each other."

Rosie spun around to face the man she never wanted to see again. "No, we can never change what happened," she said, turning the doorknob and opening the door. "I'll have my assistant call you with the name of another designer." She stalked out, not looking back.

Four

Rosie's tires squealed as she pulled away from Le-Mar's house. What was he trying to do to her? He must have tracked her down after seeing her at Mick's. She didn't buy that coincidence story for one minute.

"Men, huh," she grumbled aloud.

She turned down the radio and shook off the chill that ran through her body. God, how she'd wanted to work on that house. The excitement she'd felt had completely disappeared the minute LeMar's face had appeared on the other side of that door. It was as if someone had burst her balloon.

She ran the whole scene through her head again. LeMar had returned to Atlanta, looking less than twelve years older, and much more handsome. It was as if he'd stepped right out of her dreams. In them he hadn't abandoned her, nor had she lost the baby. They were still two college students learning about life and love from each other.

It had stopped raining, and she smiled as the sun broke through the clouds. Her mood changed from a state of total disappointment to peaceful happiness. Those old dreams were just that—old. She didn't want to revisit them, or see LeMar again. She didn't believe in backpedaling. It was time for her to move forward with her life and start thinking of the possibilities that lay ahead.

Tomorrow she'd have Neville call LeMar's secretary with the name of another designer, and that would be the end of that.

When Rosie got home, her ex-aunt-in-law, Carrie Evans was sitting on her front porch, which happened to be right next door to Rosie's. After David and Rosie had purchased their house, David had bought the house next door for his elderly aunt. She'd raised him after his parents died when he was a child. Over the years, Rosie had grown very close to Carrie, and treated her like her own grandmother. In the afternoon, Carrie liked to sit on the porch and watch the neighborhood children ride their bikes.

"Good evening, Mrs. Lady." Rosie bypassed her house and walked up to Carrie's porch.

Carrie raised her head and peered at Rosie through her bifocals. "Well now, somebody looks a little tired to me." She took a sip from the tall glass of water she held.

Holding on to the railing, Rosie pulled herself up the steps. "Try disappointed." She took a seat in one of the green wrought-iron chairs. Blooming potted plants lined the porch. On the table next to Carrie sat a pitcher of ice water.

"You know, the Lord don't put more on us than we can handle. Have faith and pray. I'm sure everything will work out."

Rosie gave her neighbor a knowing smile as she agreed with her. "True, true."

Carrie sat in her favorite seat on the side of the porch, with her feet propped up on a footstool and a copy of *Better Homes and Gardens* on her lap. No matter what problems Rosie was having, a conversation with Carrie always made her feel better.

Rosie wanted to tell Carrie about the ordeal she'd been through, but didn't know where to begin.

"How's that sister of yours?"

"Oh, she's fine. She's helping me out at the office a few days a week, and I don't know how I'm going to pay her." Rosie's worries resurfaced.

"Honey, business is right around the corner. Before you know it you'll get a call to decorate some mansion. Then you'll have enough to pay your sister and that little fella that works for you."

Hesitating for a moment, Rosie confessed. "I think I may have turned that mansion down today."

They looked at each other. Carrie set her water glass on the little round patio table and turned in her seat to face Rosie.

"Honey, you did what?"

Rosie cleared her throat. "Mind if I have some water?"

"Uh-huh, go on inside and get yourself a glass. Then come right back out here and tell me what happened." As Rosie stood to go inside, Carrie said, "I knew something was wrong the minute you came up those steps."

Inside the kitchen, Rosie grabbed a glass covered with blue and white ducks, then made her way back to the front porch.

Carrie let Rosie pour her water and sit down before staring at her over the rim of her glasses. "I'm waiting, child."

Exhaling, Rosie relaxed her shoulders. "I had an appointment today, and I didn't know until I got there that the owner was a former acquaintance of mine." She took a sip of water.

"He owns a mansion?" Carrie asked.

"Not quite a mansion, but a beautiful old home in Ansley Park. There are about three or four bedrooms, and I don't remember how many bathrooms. The house could be so elegant with a little work. The outside's in desperate need of landscaping, but the architectural detail is wonderful." Rosie's voice caught.

"Sounds nice. What's the problem?" She didn't wait for an answer. "If you have a nice house to display, the better your chances of being picked as one of those top ten Atlanta designers, right?"

Rosie raised her brow and stared toward the ceiling of the porch. "That's not exactly how it works. I'm not even going to focus on that this year. Besides, I've only been at this two years, so I don't stand a chance in hell of being selected."

Moving the magazine from her lap to the tabletop, Carrie took her feet down from the stool and looked at Rosie. "Yes, you do. Honey, you've done some beautiful work. I love that house over off Pleasant Hill where they put the pictures in *Atlanta Magazine.* That house looked like some rich folks' house over in the Caribbean somewhere with all those beautiful bright colors."

"So, you accept that job and add another creation to your credit this year. I'm telling you, you are one of the best."

Rosie shrugged. "I don't think I can work around the owner. I don't even want to see him again."

"Hmm." Carrie put her feet back up on the stool and glanced out at two little boys riding bikes past her house.

Rosie knew her neighbor well enough to know she had something to say. "Come on, let's have it."

Carrie looked over her glasses again.

"Well, you see, if this young man hires your company, that doesn't mean he gets you. Don't you have a young fella working for you who can do most of the work?"

Rosie nodded. "I'm listening."

"How many men hire you, then sit around the house and watch every move you make? None, I'm sure. This potential client does work, doesn't he?"

"Yes, he works." Rosie eyed her neighbor skeptically. She just might have something.

"If I were you, I'd take the job and have that young fella—"

"Neville. His name's Neville."

"Uh-huh, well, after you've settled everything, have that fella, Neville, deal with your friend until the job's complete. When your friend's not at home you can go in and supervise the little fella."

"Mrs. Carrie, you might have something. Neville's come far enough along to help me on this one. Not to mention, it'll be a great experience for him." Nodding, Rosie now had second thoughts about the job. Could she pull this off? Did she want to?

Carrie stood and picked up her water pitcher. "That little piece of advice will cost you, you know."

Smiling, Rosie stood to help by grabbing both glasses. The afternoon break was over. "You're something else, you know that? I'm sure you'll find a way for me to repay you."

Doreece stared at Tony, waiting for him to speak. His baby face and honey brown eyes always managed to make her weak. Why she loved this man who couldn't make a commitment, she didn't know. What she did know was that she planned on marrying him. Even his elusive ways attracted her. When she wanted him, he was available. When she didn't, he enjoyed his freedom as much as she enjoyed hers.

Tony ran his hand along the back of his neck. "Look, can't we talk about this some other time?" he said in a huff. He shoved a hand into the pocket of his lab coat.

Doreece shook her head. "You haven't returned any of my calls. Then I stopped by your house yesterday, but you weren't there. How else am I supposed to catch you?"

"I called you back. I even left a message the other day."

"Tony, you returned one call, and left a five-second message to say you were busy." She was on the verge of tears, but managed to restrain herself.

"Doreece, why do you have to hassle a brother on his job? I've never come to your job demanding things of you." His voice rose an octave. "How can you walk in here telling me what I'm gonna do when you're the one who stepped out on me? Then you said we were *just* dating, remember?" He shrugged and made a helpless gesture.

"Tony, you know I wasn't seeing anybody else, no matter what I said or did." Tears filled her eyes.

"Then what did I see you and Kent doing? I guess you tripped and fell on his lips." He lowered his voice when people walking through the lobby gave them curious glances. "Do I look like a fool to you?"

"He kissed me! I didn't initiate anything." Doreece wiped the tears she could no longer hold back.

Tony sighed and gingerly took a step closer. "Look, I know we need to talk, but this isn't the place or time to get into anything."

"When then?" she asked, with a doubtful expression on her face. "When are we going to talk about the baby?"

"Am I the father?" He pointed at himself and gave her a questioning look.

His words pierced her heart. She suppressed the urge to smack him. "In the three years we've been dating on and off, you know I haven't been intimate with anyone else. Which is more than I can say about you." She rolled her eyes and turned to leave.

Tony reached out and grabbed her arm. "Doreece, come on. I didn't mean that."

She stopped, but didn't speak for fear she'd curse him out. She couldn't even look him in the eye. One look and she'd probably have to stop herself from begging him to love her. Besides, the lobby of the medical center wasn't the place to create a scene.

Holding on to her arm, Tony said, "When I get off work this evening I'll stop by. We can talk then, okay?"

She turned and looked into his eyes. Was he serious? She nodded slowly.

"I get off at five, so I should be there by six. You know how bad traffic is."

She stared at him, not saying a word.

"I'll be there, I promise." He released her arm.

As she walked away, tears blurred her vision. She made it to her car and started the engine. Another one of his lies? God, she hoped not.

Rosie was sipping her second cup of ginseng tea when Doreece finally strolled in around ten o'clock. By then, Rosie had worked herself up into a panic over whether LeMar's secretary would call.

Doreece threw her purse on the desk and strolled over to help herself to a cup of tea. "Sorry I'm late. What's going on?"

"Nothing." Rosie tapped her fingernails against the desk and eyed the phone. It hadn't rung since Neville had called earlier.

Doreece sat down, staring into her cup. Seconds later, she jumped up, almost spilling her tea. "Rosie, I almost forgot. What happened yesterday with that house in Ansley Park?"

Rosie hadn't spoken to her since then, and now she was too nervous to go into detail. "I turned down the job."

"You what?" She pushed her cup aside and folded her arms across the desk.

Rosie sighed. "When I got there, I found out the house belonged to LeMar. He offered me the job of decorating it, but I turned him down. But after giving it some thought, I called his secretary this morning and asked her to tell him that I'd changed my mind and I'd take the job. I'm waiting for her to call me back now." Rosie exhaled.

"Wow, are you serious?" Doreece laughed.

Rosie shook her head. "It's been crazy."

"Okay, so who's Mrs. Lurlay? His wife?"

"No, his secretary. Girl, when he opened that front door, I almost fell out. I'm telling you, it was so unreal." Rosie grabbed a catalog from her desk and absently flipped through the pages.

"Was he trying to trick you by using his secretary's name?"

"He said he wasn't. He claims he didn't know who owned Yahimba Designs."

"Maybe he didn't." Doreece shrugged.

"I find that hard to believe." Rosie gave her a raised-brow smirk.

"So you turned him down, then changed your mind. Why?"

"At the time, I couldn't imagine working with him. Then, yesterday Mrs. Carrie helped me sort things out. I'm going to let Neville do most of the work."

"Do you think he's ready?" Doreece settled back into her seat.

"He's been ready. Neville's finished most of his training, and he's got a good eye."

"Then I hope we get the job. Because now is not the time for me to be unemployed. I've got to prepare for this baby." Doreece looked down at herself, rubbing the small belly that barely showed signs of pregnancy.

Since Doreece brought the baby up, Rosie decided to ask a few questions. "Did you have a talk with Tony yet?"

Doreece raised her chin. "Yes, and he's coming over tonight so we can talk more."

"Good. I hope he plans to support that baby. Don't let him walk away from his responsibility." Rosie pushed her chair back and stood.

"He's not going to do that."

Rosie pulled the file on her next job and returned to her desk. She couldn't concentrate because she had too much on her mind. Not only was she nervous about LeMar, but Doreece's situation bothered her as well.

"Doreece, have you thought about things like insurance, and who's going to care for the child while you work? Can you afford day care?"

Doreece went to pour out her tea. "I said Tony's coming by tonight, and we'll discuss all that."

"So you've cleared up that mess about Kent?"

Spinning around with her teacup in hand, Doreece gave her sister the evil eye. "Rosie, you know nothing happened between us."

"Then why on earth did you try to make Tony think it did?"

"I wanted him to know that somebody else was interested in me if he didn't get his act together. I didn't know I was pregnant then."

"So your plan backfired and now he thinks you've had sex with Kent and you're having his baby?"

"Yes, and he's wrong. I'm a harmless big flirt, and everybody knows that."

Rosie shrugged and flopped down in her seat. "Doreece, you shouldn't play games like that. People get hurt. Tony probably doesn't know what to think."

"Oh, he knows better." She set her cup down, stomped over to her desk, and snatched her purse.

"Actions speak louder than words. He knows what he saw you doing. You went about that the wrong way."

"Rosie, you're supposed to be on my side."

"I am on your side. However, I want you to see that what you did was childish and immature."

"I need some air, and I need to talk to somebody who's more supportive. I'm taking a break. I'll be back."

Rosie stood and rushed around her desk to catch Doreece, but the phone rang.

"A break! You just came in," she called after her. She turning slowly and stared at the ringing phone. There he was! On the other end of that phone was the man she should have married. The man she was supposed to marry, until tragedy had struck.

After the third ring, she reached over and grabbed the receiver.

Five

In a controlled and smooth voice Rosie answered the phone. "Yahimba Designs, may I help you?"

The sound of menacing laughter crept through the phone, followed by a deep raspy whisper. "I know all about it."

"What? Who is this?" Rosie barely made out the sound on the other end of the phone. A chill ran through her.

"I said, who is this?" she demanded.

"You know who it is." Again the person whispered.

She racked her brain trying to make out the voice on the other end. "Is this—"

Suddenly, the line went dead.

She hung up the phone. *What the hell was that about?* Sitting back, she crossed her arms and stared at the phone. It could have been some kids. Or maybe Neville was playing with her. But it didn't sound like his voice.

The phone rang again. Rosie jumped and grabbed the receiver. This time she listened for a few seconds before saying anything. "Hello, Yahimba Designs," she finally said with caution.

"May I speak with Mrs. Wright?"

The perky voice on the other end of the phone was a pleasant change.

"Speaking. May I help you?"

"Hello, Mrs. Wright. This is Brenda Lurlay, Mr. Reed's secretary, and I'm returning your call."

Rosie's heart could have leaped from her chest as she adjusted herself to sit straight in the chair. "Yes. Thank you for getting back to me."

"I gave Mr. Reed your message, and he would like to set up a time that's convenient for you to begin."

Yes! Rosie jabbed her fist in the air. She hadn't lost the job after all. "Let me see, I believe I have an opening later this week." She flipped through her scarcely filled calendar pages. "I can fit him in on Wednesday morning."

"He has a conference call at ten o'clock that morning. Could you make it early, say eight A.M.?"

Rosie penciled it in. "Eight o'clock is fine. Brenda, may I ask you something?"

"Sure."

"We like to see how our advertising dollars are working. Can you tell me how Mr. Reed heard about our office?"

"Uh—I'm not quite sure, but I think one of his coworkers, Grace, recommended your office."

"Thank you. Well, tell Mr. Reed I'll see him on Wednesday." Butterflies danced in Rosie's stomach as she hung up the phone.

Once this job began, there would be no getting around discussing her past with LeMar. Even if she gave Neville most of the work, she knew that day was inevitable.

At six A.M. Wednesday, Rosie rolled over and hit the snooze button. She normally didn't get up until eight A.M. and didn't arrive in the office before ten, unless she had an early appointment. She finally rose at six-fifteen, and dragged herself into the bathroom to hazily go through her morning ritual. Standing inside her walk-in closet, she stared at the clothes, willing something to jump out at her. Black. Jackets, slacks, skirts, dresses . . . there was too much black. Until today she hadn't actually noticed how much black her closet held. For Christ's sake, she was a decorator. Her closet should have more color.

She settled on a black pantsuit with a beige blouse, then played with her hair for almost thirty minutes. Finally, she settled on a cool upsweep.

The minute she stepped outside, it began sprinkling. Fortunately, she always kept an umbrella in her car, so she didn't worry.

By the time she pulled up to LeMar's house, the sprinkle had become a monsoon. She collected her umbrella from the backseat and peered out the window. She hated the rain. If she had her choice, she'd never leave the house on rainy days.

"Well, here goes," she said as she eased the door open and pushed her umbrella out. So much rain traveled through the crack in the door that she almost changed her mind. "It's just water," she told herself and kept moving. In a pair of black pumps, with her purse and tote bag held close to her body, Rosie jumped out of the car and raced for the front porch. Her umbrella took a beating as the wind whipped it around, but she held the metal handle tightly.

Before she reached the porch, she lost the fight. The rain slapped her face as the wind snatched her umbrella and sent it toppling down the street. Thankful for the large covered porch, she leaned against the wall, trying to catch her breath. She looked down at her wet clothes, which clung to her body. The umbrella had provided little protection in this weather.

To her surprise, the front door swung open.

"Okay, okay, okay," LeMar repeated, then looked at her with wide eyes.

Rosie wanted to crawl into a hole and die. Her back was pressed against the doorbell. Water dripped from her nose, and through wet eyelashes she could see a little smile on his face.

"Are you going to let me in, or would you like to come out and join me?" she asked through clenched teeth. She couldn't believe he was laughing at her. It had taken her forever to get dressed this morning, and now this.

The smile on LeMar's face turned into a huge grin as he stroked his mustache. He motioned her in. "You should have blown the horn. I've got an umbrella. I would have come out and gotten you."

She walked past him, cutting her eyes. "I had an umbrella. The wind carried it down the street for me." She stood there, dripping onto the hardwood floor.

He closed the door. "Let me grab you a towel." He dashed into the hall bathroom, then returned with a hand towel.

She wiped her face first, then her purse. "May I use your bathroom?"

"Sure, help yourself."

Once in the bathroom, she closed the door behind her and grabbed another towel. She looked at her dewy face in the mirror. Right now she didn't look too professional; her upsweep was now lying on her shoulders and in her face. Pulling her makeup pouch from her purse, she tried to repair what the rain had damaged. She took the hairpins out and tucked her hair behind her ears. With the towel, she sponged her clothes down as best she could.

Before she exited, she took one last look in the

mirror. "Hideous!" However, she couldn't let the fact that she was wet and uncomfortable get in the way of business.

She followed the sound of the television and found LeMar in the den. A special news bulletin was reporting on the rainstorm and traffic accidents.

"Thank you, I believe I'm ready to start now," she said from the doorway.

He rose from the couch and turned the volume down with the remote. "Well, you don't look like you're about to melt anymore."

The provocative look he gave her caused her to look away. She tried to suppress it, but felt herself blush. "I'm a little drier now, thanks."

An awkward silence hung in the air. She saw the guy who got drunk one night after a football game, and serenaded her in front of all his friends. For a man who couldn't carry a tune, he'd still managed to bring her to tears. However, this wasn't exactly the same guy. He had matured into a more distinguished and sexy man.

"Okay, I guess we can start at the beginning. I'm glad you changed your mind about the job." He walked back into the foyer.

"So am I," she said, trying to shake her thoughts of the past. As he walked past, the smell of his cologne tickled her senses.

"If you want, you can leave your things in the den."

"Thanks." She pulled a steno pad from her tote and left the tote bag and purse on the couch.

He stopped and looked up the stairs. "I'd like to start there." He pointed toward the top.

The wallpaper had yellowed and the paint was peeling. The area was in desperate need of a little attention.

"When you walk in the front door, that's the first thing you see. That wallpaper has got to go. The whole place needs a good paint job."

"I see what you mean." She nodded. "Let's take a walk around the house and discuss what you'd like to do, and how you see the house transforming."

"I purchased this house knowing I'd have to redo it. I like the structure, but not the wallpaper or all this dated French-looking stuff. I need to update the place a little. And I'd like an office on this floor. The former owner had one upstairs. Other than that, I don't have much of a clue."

How did she know that was the case? "That's fine. Most people aren't too sure what they want. I'll take a look and offer some suggestions. In a couple of days I'll give you an estimate, and we can iron out more details then."

"Sounds good."

He gave her the grand tour. Rosie's eyes grew wider as he talked about the rooms he wanted enlarged and all the design changes that were needed. A billiard table in the basement meant knocking down some walls. This was going to be a major job, and she could certainly use Neville's assistance, and LeMar's money.

LeMar took every opportunity he could to watch Rosie. She looked as youthful and beautiful as she had in college. Only now, she had a sex appeal that she hadn't had before. Every move she made enticed him. Earlier, when she entered the den, he liked the alluring way she had her hair swept behind her ears. Being around her might not be as difficult as he'd originally thought. He could possibly forgive her for the past, and move on.

"Is this going to be a guest bedroom?" she asked as she entered another half-empty room.

"This one, and the one next door. I figured I'd keep them pretty simple. This is my old bedroom furniture. It's more than fifteen years old, but it's still good. I'm sure you can make it look almost new."

"Yeah, these four-poster beds are classics. I'd keep this furniture for sure. We can accessorize in here." She loved the expensive mahogany wood pieces he'd brought with him.

He left the guest room. "Down here in my room I purchased a new bedroom set. The furniture's cool, but I don't like the bathroom." At the end of the hall he walked into the master bedroom.

She walked in behind him, totally taken aback by the sheer size of the room. There was a sitting area with a fireplace across from the bed. His bedroom furniture didn't begin to fill up the room.

LeMar walked across the room to the bathroom and turned on the light. She followed him.

"See. There's an old tub, which is too little for me. I thought about a large whirlpool tub. Do you think one will fit in here?"

She could picture a huge tub sitting under the window with them inside, his legs wrapped around her body. *Oh, God help me.* What was she thinking? "Yeah—uh, you can find one to fit no problem. We can have it tiled in, too."

He nodded. "That'll work."

"LeMar, if you don't mind me asking, what are you going to do with all the space in this house? It's rather large for a single man."

"I know. This is what I wanted, though. My first house in D.C. was so small it felt like an apartment. This feels like a home."

"It's certainly that."

"I might move my mother down in a few years. If I do, I've got plenty of room for her."

"That's true. You've got room to move a whole family down." She laughed.

"There's nobody in D.C. but my mom. I plan on making Atlanta my home for quite a while. That is, if things work out for me. I missed Atlanta when I was in D.C."

Rosie grinned. "It's a little cheaper than D.C., that's for sure. You get more for your money here."

"Which is why I had to jump on this house. I couldn't believe I got such a good deal. And I'm not far from downtown or work, which is a plus."

"Yeah, this is a good location," she said, leaning against the door frame.

"Well, that about does it for upstairs. Most of the work is downstairs."

They left the bedrooms, and he escorted her down the hall to the back stairs.

"So, how's your business?" He wanted to know something about her life.

"Just fine."

"How long have you been operating?"

"Two years."

LeMar wasn't getting anywhere with her short answers. He wanted to know some things about her. The back stairs led into the kitchen.

All this talking had made him thirsty. "Would you like something to drink?" he offered, opening a squeaky cabinet door for glasses. The cabinets were painted white, and showed years of use.

"Sure, a glass of water would be fine."

He poured two glasses of water and walked over to the kitchen table. His glass-top dinette set looked out of place with the more traditional kitchen decor. He sat down, hoping Rosie would take a break and relax with him.

She did.

He looked around the room. "One thing I'd like to do is tear this kitchen apart. Get rid of those white cabinets and all the outdated appliances."

"Yes, this kitchen does need updating. By remodeling you can make better use of some of this space."

"I'm curious, what does an interior designer's house look like?" Finally an open-ended question. She'd have to elaborate. He smiled, happy with himself.

"It's a work in progress. It's comfortable, but I'm never finished with it. And it has taken me years to get things where they are today. I like so many styles that I keep changing everything. I think it's important to fill your home with things that make you feel good. So, I've finally settled on an African-Moroccan mix of sorts. Surrounding myself with things from the motherland makes me feel good."

"Yeah, I'd like a little African influence, too. I've got several pieces of African art that I haven't unpacked yet, and some sculptures I brought back from the Caribbean that I'd like to mix in."

"You've got a nice traditional base here to work with. I think we can mix in a little of Africa nicely."

"I'd like to see your home sometime—that is, if it's okay with you?" If there was a man in her life, now was the time to tell him.

She finished her water and pushed the glass across the table toward him. "I've got a photo book I carry around. I'll bring it next time."

That wasn't exactly what he had in mind. "Sure, bring it by." He heard the ticking of the clock and looked down at his watch. Time was flying, and he had to get to work.

"You have a meeting this morning, don't you?" she asked, standing.

"Yeah, so I guess we'd better hurry and finish down here and in the basement."

This meeting wasn't going the way LeMar had hoped. He wanted to discuss their past and get that out of the way. Instead, he was talking to the only woman he'd ever truly loved as if they'd just met.

They ended the tour in the den an hour after they'd started. "Rosie, I haven't told you, but it's really good to see you again. You look great." He hadn't forgotten the pain she'd caused him years ago. He just didn't want to dwell on it.

"Thank you, it's good seeing you, too." She managed to avoid eye contact.

"Is it really?" His voice was laced with curiosity.

"What?"

"Good to see me, too? I didn't get that impression the last time you were here. I was surprised when you called. Pleased, but surprised," he clarified.

"LeMar, what happened between us is just where it should be—in the past. Forgive and forget is my motto. I've come to terms with the past. Now I'm here to help you with this wonderful house you've purchased." She looked away.

"I'm glad you feel that way," he replied skeptically.

"Did I tell you that I've always admired this house? I met the former owners once." She eased away from him and walked over to examine the drapes.

"No, I don't believe you'd mentioned it." He did notice she'd changed subjects as she gracefully strolled around the room. He took a seat on the arm of the couch and watched her. If she believed in her own forgive-and-forget theory, why did she storm out on him last time? Maybe she *forgot* to forgive him.

"This is my first time seeing the inside. This house

really has character. There are some nice touches added here. Like those antique chandeliers. Let me know if you decide to get rid of any of them." She pulled back the drapes and checked out the windows. "Yeah, you've got a great investment here."

There was a knock at the front door before LeMar could respond. "Excuse me, I'll be right back."

Rosie folded her steno pad and put it back in her tote bag. Since he had company, this was a perfect time for her to leave. She left the den and headed toward the front door.

"Well, if it isn't Rosie from Clark Atlanta. How you doing, baby?" Eddie walked up to Rosie and extended his hand.

She offered a limp handshake while gritting her teeth. "Eddie, what a surprise." She would have rather walked in horse manure than be bothered with this man. Now her hands felt dirty.

"You two get reacquainted, I'll be right back." LeMar ran upstairs.

Eddie walked past Rosie, leering at her from head to toe. "I bet you're surprised to see me. Didn't know me and your boy were still hanging, did ya?"

"No, I didn't."

He glanced up the stairs. "Yeah, we're still cool." He looked back at Rosie. "I see you guys are still cool, too?"

"He hired me to redesign his house. It's business."

"Yeah," he said, sucking his teeth. "I bet you two got plenty of business. Or unfinished business."

Rosie just shook her head. What was he getting at? "Let's just say that's none of *your* business." He knew she didn't like him, and she never had.

"I think so, since I live here, too." He leaned against the hall table and cut Rosie a wicked grin.

She was speechless. At the sound of footsteps, she looked up and saw LeMar coming down the stairs. "You two best friends yet?"

Six

Eddie smiled at Rosie and shook his head. "We're getting reacquainted." He turned to LeMar, who stood at the bottom of the steps. "So you're gonna get this place fixed up?"

"Yeah, it'll look like a new house when Rosie finishes with it." He gave her an affirming smile. "Right?"

"That's right. You won't know the place once I'm finished. And you'll love it." She directed her answer to LeMar, refusing to look at Eddie.

This whole scene reminded her of something from the past. LeMar and Eddie, together again like Frick and Frack. The three of them stood there, smiling awkwardly at one another.

"I'll let you guys get back to work. Rosie, good seeing you again. And I'll look forward to seeing you around. Later." Eddie headed back to the kitchen.

LeMar handed Rosie his business card. "Here— that's my work number in case you need to get in touch with me."

She took the card and read his title: INFORMATION MANAGEMENT, SOUTHEASTERN REGION MANAGER. There were his phone, fax, and cellular numbers. Pretty good job, she guessed. His ambition was one of the things that had attracted her in the first place. Here he was, barely thirty years old and already a regional manager of something.

"Look, I'm sorry about him." He pointed toward the kitchen. "I remember how you guys got along."

She rolled her eyes. "I didn't know he'd be here, but I guess I should have." What did LeMar see in the guy? Eddie got kicked out of college, spent a little time in jail, and tried to lie his way out of everything. They weren't exactly in the same class.

LeMar tilted his head and gave her a lopsided smile. "Come on, give the guy a break. He's all right."

Oh . . . how his smiles made her weak in the knees. She almost agreed with him. She had to turn away to get her head together. Then, she gestured vaguely toward the kitchen. "He said he lives here, is that right?"

"He'll be around for a week or two, that's all. Don't worry, he won't get in your way."

She put his business card in her purse. "Well, I've gotta run. I can get back on Friday with the contract if that's good for you? Then I can get started."

He ran a finger along his temple. "I know I've got a department meeting that morning. How about Friday evening? I can cut out early."

"That's fine. I'll see you Friday evening then."

"Okay—and, uh, thanks again for taking the job. I know it was a hard decision to make."

She could see the genuine concern in his eyes. "It was a tough decision to make, but I've had to make tougher. I can work around anything."

"Good, but I wasn't talking about Eddie. I meant me."

This was the type of conversation she had to avoid. "I know what you meant. Don't worry. I'm a big girl, I can handle it."

* * *

After the pressure of that visit, getting drenched, and running into Fast Eddie, Rosie needed a little stress relief. She had gone home to change clothes, but decided to get in a quick workout. It took her less than three minutes to change and hurry to her basement, which doubled as a workout room.

Her 1980s mix of music from Prince to Madonna served as an instant energy booster. She blasted the volume on her CD player and tried to pedal thoughts of LeMar out of her head. Her mind ran faster than the bike. She needed a plan for dealing with LeMar and Eddie.

Thirty minutes later, she climbed down off the bike, toweled off, and called Neville.

"Rosie, what happened to you Friday night?" he asked in an anxious tone.

"I'm sorry. I'd planned to come, but things got out of hand and I forgot."

"You forgot? Girl, you missed a great party. Kitty was so proud of herself. You should have seen her. She spent most of the night patting herself on the back."

Rosie laughed at Neville's accurate description of one of her design classmates. After graduation, Kitty Jackson had landed a position with a prestigious design firm, just as most of Rosie's white classmates had. The owner of Kitty's firm was her lover, and twenty years her senior. With his backing, she'd managed to open offices in Atlanta, Chicago, and now South Beach, Florida.

"Did she remind everybody of how many locations she now has?"

"Of course," he said with a popping sarcastic tone.

"Neville, let's quit player hating. It's really good

she found somebody to help her, and I guess we should be happy for her."

"Honey, if she didn't rub it in people's faces, I would be happy for her. When Roy got the invite, we knew it was going to be a look-at-how-successful-I-am party. You know how she has to be the center of attention."

"I'll call her tomorrow and apologize for not showing up. I'm sure she'll enjoy telling me what I missed. Neville, about work . . . I've got something for you."

"I thought you wanted me to take a little break?"

"I did, but something came up, so now you don't have to. We've got a huge job."

"Wonderful, where is it?"

"In Ansley Park. It's a beautiful old traditional home that needs a lot of renovating and design work."

"Hey, that's great. Maybe this is the beginning of an upswing."

"Let's hope so. Hey, do you remember when we talked about you taking on more responsibility?"

"Yeah, a couple of months back when we thought we had that hotel deal. But that fell through, right?"

"It did, but I'm thinking of letting you run with this one. It'll mean more hours instead of fewer. The client is interested in African influences. I don't think he wants anything too heavy—a few subtle touches throughout the house. We can look around together and work up a design board, but I want you to handle the bulk of the work."

"Rosie, thank you. I really appreciate the opportunity. Wow, Ansley Park! This is a designer's dream. Those houses have so much character and style."

Rosie chuckled. "I'm glad you're excited. Are you available Friday evening to visit the client with me?"

"Man, I wish I was. When you told me to take a

break, I took on a painting job. It should be complete by Saturday at the latest."

She thought for a moment. That meant she had to return alone. However, she couldn't afford to wait.

"Okay, don't worry about Friday. I'll take care of it. I'll get with you afterward and go over all the particulars. Thanks, Neville."

"No, thank you. This is a great opportunity."

"Rosie, I need you to take a look at this invoice." Doreece walked over to Rosie with her head buried in the paperwork.

"Doreece, I've got forty-five minutes before I have to meet Nate Williams downtown. Can you handle whatever it is?"

"So, he decided to be a sponsor?"

"Yes, and I'm meeting him to pick up the check. Colony Homes is almost complete with the house. I need to start pulling it together."

"That's great. How long before the family moves in?"

"The move-in date is set for mid-July, which means we've got almost two months, and I still need more sponsors. I'm cutting it close this year."

"Man, this is a fun project. You get to go out and decorate this place anyway you want to. It's like when we were kids playing house."

"That's why I love my job," Rosie said with a smile.

The phone rang and Rosie looked at her watch. She didn't have time to do anything but leave. She let Doreece grab the phone while she grabbed her purse.

Doreece stood up and waved her back. "One moment, sir, I think I can catch her before she leaves."

Rosie hoped it wasn't Nate.

"It's Mr. Williams. He wanted to catch you before you left." She shrugged and held out the receiver.

"He probably wants to reschedule." She tried to be optimistic, but as she took the phone, she had a feeling this was going to be bad news.

"Hello, Nate. I was on my way to meet you."

"Yeah, that's why I called. I sat down with my partner and discussed your project. He agrees it's a great project and something we should be involved in."

But . . .

"However, I'm sorry to say my partner has committed the company to another charity project. We won't be able to help out this year after all."

She wanted to reach through the phone and slap him. All the time she'd wasted pitching the idea to him. She was so sure he'd say yes.

"Nathan, I'm sorry to hear that. I really needed your sponsorship this year. If the financial contribution is too much, maybe you can donate a few pieces of furniture?" At this point, she'd take anything she could get.

"I'm afraid we can't. Since you do this every year, maybe we can participate next year. We've already overextended ourselves this year."

"I'm sorry we won't be working together. I'll look forward to your participation next year." She didn't want to burn any bridges, but she wanted to slam the phone in his ear.

"You should stop by the store sometime and we can discuss it. Maybe we can do lunch?"

"Right now I'm afraid I'll be too busy trying to secure another sponsor," she said with a sharp edge to her voice.

"Yeah, I'm real sorry about that."

"Well, I'll send you some information about next year. And thanks again for calling me before I went all the way downtown." She hung up, not giving him time to respond.

Doreece leaned against her table with her arms crossed. "He's probably mad because you didn't go out with him."

"Then he'll stay mad. I'm not going to date him in exchange for his sponsorship. And he still had the nerve to come on to me after turning down the project."

"God, what a sleaze."

"He's worse. I'm too much of a lady to call him out of his name. He's lucky." She sat there stewing for a few minutes.

"Doreece, scratch their name off the list of possible sponsors. I'm never dealing with him again."

"Good for you."

"Now I have to find some furniture."

"What happens if you don't get a sponsor for the furniture?"

"The family stays in a shelter until I do. But that's not going to be a problem. I'll get the furniture." She grabbed her purse and got back up.

"Where are you going now?"

"To find an even better furniture store that wants to help. I'll see you this afternoon." She left the office, determined to secure all the furniture she needed.

Friday evening, Rosie pulled up to LeMar's with a contract and an estimate in her planner. The meeting should take no more than thirty minutes, she guessed. All she needed was his signature and a check for the deposit. She hoped Eddie wasn't there.

It took LeMar a while to answer the door. When he did, he had a short white terry cloth wrap around his waist, exposing his chiseled chest. His damp black hair shined as he stood there glistening.

Her jaw dropped. She noticed the oblong scar on his chest he'd gotten as a child. She remembered his story detailing the fight. Then she slowly lowered her gaze to his long, solid muscular legs. The blood rushed to her face as her fingertips tingled. She stood there awestruck while her gaze traveled back to his face.

She held up her planner. "I've got that contract."

He took a step back and glanced down. "I'm sorry, I was trying to hurry. Come on in." He moved aside and motioned her in before he continued.

"I had a rather rough day, and my meeting ran over." He closed the door and walked toward the stairs. "Have a seat in the den. I'll throw some clothes on and be right back." He disappeared up the stairs.

Smiling, she moseyed into the den and sat on the couch. Soft jazz filled the room. Thank God, he was dressing. She didn't want to admit it to herself, but for heaven's sake, she could watch him parade around in that towel all evening. What a body! She hadn't been that close to an almost naked man in more than two years.

However, if this was some ploy to entice her into something, he'd better think again. She could look without touching. "Sorry, mister, that won't work here," she declared.

"What won't work?" LeMar asked as he entered the room.

Startled, she bolted up from the couch. He stood in the doorway, casually dressed in a gold-and-black warm-up suit, with no shoes or socks.

"Oh, nothing. I was thinking out loud," she said matter-of-factly. To make it through this evening—and this job—she needed to be as professional as possible, and not think about his sexy legs. She sat back down.

LeMar took a seat opposite the couch and rubbed his palms together. "Well, let's see what you've got."

"I won't take up much of your time." She pulled out the contract.

"Take your time, I've got all evening."

She glanced up and gave him a wary look as he smiled. "Here's an estimate and my contract. Look them over, and we can discuss anything you'd like. You'll see the deposit required is noted at the bottom."

She caught a whiff of his cologne as he looked over the contract and she picked at her nails. She hadn't purchased men's cologne in so long that she didn't recognize the fragrance. He smelled good, looked good, and had a good job, all the qualities of a great catch, as her best friend, Sharon, would say. It was just too bad that he wasn't trustworthy, or rather that he hadn't been.

"Uh-huh, looks good to me. If you have a pen, I'll sign it and write you a check." He laid the contract on the coffee table.

"You didn't read it!" She looked at him as if he'd fallen from the sky. He couldn't have done more than scan the document.

"No need, I trust you to use your best judgment. I don't do much entertaining, and I live a modest and comfortable life. You know me." He took the pen from her and signed his name.

"I don't know what to say, but I appreciate all the confidence. If you have any concerns or questions at all, feel free to call me."

He let her separate the copies of the contract. "I forgot my checkbook. I'll be right back." He left the den and returned a few minutes later, handing over his check.

He took his copy of the contract and folded it. "I'm sure it's going to be fun working with you. Just like old times, almost." He held out his hand to her.

She stood and gave him a firm handshake. "Decorating is always fun for me, and I hope not to inconvenience you too much." She placed the contract in her planner. Time to exit stage left.

"So what's next?"

"We need to pick out your colors, and then start selecting cabinetry and everything else. We'll do it in stages."

"Great." He reached into his pants pocket. "Oh, I almost forgot." He pulled out a shiny gold key and offered it to her. "Here's the key to the house. Brenda told me you'd need it to get in."

She reached for the key, but he held on to it. "Thank you," she said while gently pulling on it. What type of game was he playing now?

"This house means a lot to me. You'll treat it with kid gloves, won't you?" Before she could answer or let go of the key, he continued. "Just don't discard it like you did me. My house is like my heart, damaged and in need of repair." He let go and gave her half a smile.

His revelation caught her off guard. Her heartbeat accelerated as she stuffed the key into her purse. God, no. Why was he going there?

LeMar had a wounded look in his eyes. She'd seen that look numerous times. For a brief moment she started to tell him how much she'd regretted the way they'd lost contact over the years. However, the memory of her miscarriage flashed across her mind. A claustrophobic feeling engulfed her, and she suddenly needed air.

"Your house is going to be beautiful, but I'm afraid I can't help you with your heart."

He shook his head and gave her a knowing smile. "I'm sorry. That was way out of line. Forget I said it." With his hands shoved into his pockets, he walked around her and toward the front door.

Rosie followed him, eager to vacate the premises.

He stopped short, causing her to stumble over the rug. She fell forward, but he caught her. His hand slid around her waist, and he was careful not to topple over with her.

She was off balance and grabbed hold of his arms to right herself. "LeMar, what are you . . ." His lips pressed gently against hers before she could finish her sentence. The urge to return his kiss and revel in his embrace was so strong that she had to fight with herself to push him away.

"What do you think you're doing?" she shrieked, finally able to pull away. She pressed the back of her hand to her mouth as she leaned against the wall and glared at him.

He backed into the opposite wall. "I'm sorry—I didn't want you to fall. Then you were so close, I couldn't resist." He cast his eyes downward.

She ran her hand through her hair. "LeMar, is this gonna work out? I'm your designer, not your girlfriend."

"I know. It's just that seeing you unleashed all these unresolved feelings I have. Maybe we need to talk." He shrugged his shoulders.

Rosie held up her hand, palm out, desperate to stop him from talking. "LeMar, don't do this. I don't want to discuss the past with you. I left school, got married, and went on with my life. I'm sure you went on with yours, too." She pulled away from the wall.

He looked down at the gold band on her finger.

Why hadn't he noticed it before? He'd made an ass of himself. Maybe Eddie was right.

"If I'm going to take this job, we have to keep everything on a professional level."

He pulled himself together. "I owe you an apology. It won't ever happen again. I promise. I hope it doesn't change your mind about the job. I'll see you tomorrow morning, won't I?"

She twisted her mouth and stared at his outstretched hand. "We'll see you tomorrow." She shook his hand, then finally made her exit.

He watched her walk out to the car. *You're married, but are you happy?*

Seven

Rosie walked into the house ready to fall across the bed and crash. This had not been one of her better days. She didn't even feel like working out this evening. Her system had taken a shock that she needed time to get over.

She walked into her bedroom, kicked off her shoes, and slipped out of her clothes. Beside her bed was a table full of some of her favorite scented candles. She lit two of them, then fluffed the pillows on her bed. Releasing a heavy sigh, she sat down and fell back into the pillows. Her eyelids slowly closed, then opened quickly at the shrill ring of the phone.

"Hello."

"Have I got good news for you," Doreece's cheerful voice sang through the phone.

"Great, let me have it." Mentally exhausted, Rosie couldn't muster too much excitement.

"Okay—you know I went to pick up the linens for the Colony House. But you'll never guess who I ran into."

"You're right, I'll never guess, so who?"

"Touchy, touchy. I met Phillip Hamilton. He used to play basketball for the Atlanta Hawks. I told him all about your project and asked if he was interested in being a sponsor and guess what?"

"Don't make me guess." The stress of the day still consumed Rosie.

"He's interested. He'll be getting in touch with us. You know he just purchased a house in Riverdale, Georgia. I heard it's huge, and who knows, maybe he needs a designer."

"Doreece, remind me to kiss you when I see you. That's the kind of good news I needed. You're just a little marketing machine."

"Hey, that's what you hired me for. By the way, I think he's single, too. I saw his car. He drives a Lexus, and—"

"Would you stop it? I'm looking for another sponsor, not a man."

"Well, I think I've found you a sponsor, and possibly a man. If you play your cards right. He's cute, too."

"Okay, enough of that, what did you do with the linens?"

"Oh, I took them over to the Colony House. Are we still going shopping tomorrow to finish off the bathrooms?"

"Yes, and we've got about two months to finish everything."

"Hey, after we finish tomorrow, can we stop and look at some baby clothes? I've got this urge to buy something pretty and pink. Do you think that means it's going to be a girl?"

Rosie hesitated a moment. "Sorry, but I don't think so. We can stop after we finish shopping." She wasn't too enthused about being around baby clothes. For months the sight of babies or baby clothes upset her. Maybe now she could bring herself to browse without crying.

"Speaking of babies, did you and Tony talk yet?"

"He had to leave town on business. But, we will."

"So, he lied to you again?"

"Stop being so negative will you. He'll come around, you'll see. He just needs time."

Rosie hated to see her sister going through this. "Okay, okay, I'll back off. I just hope you know what you're doing."

Friday night, LeMar sat in his gym clothes watching Fox Sports Net. He switched to ESPN, then back to Fox, not sure which ball game to watch. The problem was, he didn't want to watch any game. He wanted to have something better to do.

He hadn't been in a relationship in more than a year. And he'd never felt for any woman what he'd felt for Rosie. He couldn't get her off his mind.

"What's your problem?"

LeMar looked up and saw Eddie standing in the doorway. Dressed in an old suit with large lapels and buttons, he looked like he was going to a seventies party.

"I don't have a problem."

"Then why are you laying in on a Friday night instead of going out?"

LeMar shrugged. "I'm not big on nightclubs."

"What? Since when?"

Stretching his arms over his head, he responded, "I feel more like going to bed. I didn't leave the office until eight-thirty. Man, after working all day, I don't want to go out."

"So when does your girl start her decorating?"

"She actually started last Wednesday. You weren't here but she did all her prep work. She'll be back next week sometime." They were both silent for a few minutes, then the cheering from the television audience caught their attention. With his eyes glued to the screen, LeMar broke the silence. "You know, you were right about her."

Eddie walked into the room, sat on the edge of the chair, and stared at the television. "Right about what?"

"She's married."

Eddie's gaze turned from the television to LeMar. "She is?"

"Yeah, isn't that what you told me?"

Eddie shrugged. "I took a wild guess. I wasn't sure."

"Well, she is. It's no big deal. As long as she helps with the house, that's good enough for me."

"Sure it is," Eddie mocked sarcastically.

"Speaking of women . . . how's everything going with you and your lady? You still in the doghouse?" What he really wanted to know was when Eddie would be leaving.

Turning down his lips and shaking his head, Eddie responded. "I'll never understand women. One minute they're all over you, the next they've got their hand out. Do I look like the Bank of America?"

"What did she ask for, rent money?" LeMar chuckled.

"Try that and all her bills. Then I'm supposed to take her out on top of that. Man, women don't understand about hard times. Right now, I just don't have the money. Besides, she works."

"You never told me her name. And how long have you guys been together?"

"We've been hanging out for about five or six months." He stood and reached into his pocket. "But I'm cutting that loose. She's looking for a sugar daddy, and I ain't the one. Right now I've got to make some money."

Ready to fall asleep on the couch, LeMar yawned before asking, "How do you plan on doing that?"

"Me and some guys running a card game tonight. By the way, I need another favor."

"What's that?"

"Can you loan me a little cash? I'll pay it back after the game tonight."

LeMar looked up at Eddie standing with his hands in his pockets and was certain that this favor was the only reason he'd stopped in the den before going out. He shook his head. "Not to play cards with, I don't have that kind of money. Is that how you've been making your money?"

"A little here and there. You know, a brother's gotta make some money somehow."

The doorbell rang and LeMar got up from the couch. Eddie backed out into the hallway. "That's for me. My car's not running right now." He turned around and went to answer the door.

LeMar walked out into the hallway to see who was at his door. Eddie opened the door and a guy stepped into the foyer. He wasn't one of their mutual friends.

"Hey, what's up, man? You ready?" he asked Eddie as he walked in.

They whispered about something before Eddie said, "Yeah, dude, let me get with ya, I'll be right out."

The man looked past Eddie at LeMar, and LeMar didn't like him on sight. He had a rather shady look.

Eddie turned around and introduced them.

"LeMar, this is my man, Dru." He didn't let Dru in any further than the foyer.

Dru nodded, then looked around. "Nice place you got here."

"Thanks."

"Yo, man, I'm gonna grab a smoke. I'll be waiting in the car." Dru nodded again and turned to leave.

"I'll be with ya in a sec." Eddie turned to LeMar. "Yo, man, you sure you can't spot me a few dollars?"

Ignoring the voice of reason in his head, LeMar pulled a ten-dollar bill from his pocket. "That's it, man. And we need to sit down and talk about this card game."

Eddie shoved the money into his pocket. "Thanks, I'll get this back to ya."

"Where did you meet that dude anyway?" Dru looked as if he'd lived a rough life. He had hard features and glassy eyes, which reminded LeMar of someone on drugs.

"Dru's cool," Eddie replied, shrugging.

"Don't let Dru get you locked up, because I'm not bailing you out. What you need is a real job, not a hustle."

"Everything's cool. We're just playing cards. Look, I gotta run. Catch you later."

LeMar closed the front door behind Eddie and returned to the den. He stretched out on the couch again. In twelve years he'd kept in touch with Eddie on and off, but he didn't know how drastic of a turn his life had taken. He was learning more and more about his buddy every day.

A week later, minor renovation work had begun on LeMar's house. He and Rosie had worked out most of the details. She supervised everything in the beginning, then left Neville on his own to continue.

Neville met the contractors at LeMar's house around eight o'clock in the morning. Once he explained the details for the outside, Neville went inside and started taking down the kitchen cabinets. A few minutes into his work, the kitchen door flew open.

"What the hell's going on in here?" Eddie stormed in, ready for a fight.

"I'm sorry. I didn't realize anyone was home." Neville climbed down from his ladder. "I'm Neville Broady. I work for Yahimba Designs and we're remodeling—"

"I know about the remodeling, but what the hell are you doing here? Where's Rosie?" he bellowed, still half asleep.

Neville cleared his throat. It wasn't going to be a pleasant morning with this guy around. "She's working on another project this morning."

Eddie walked over and opened the refrigerator door. When he didn't find what he was looking for, he slammed the door. "Damn, not one beer."

"Did my banging wake you?" Neville attempted to strike up a conversation. Eddie stared at him when he passed, as though something nasty was under his shoe. Neville moved over and put his tools down. He didn't know if he should continue working or join the contractors outside.

"If I'm disturbing you, I can wait a little while and come back."

Eddie scratched his head, still staring at Neville. "You some kind of decorator, too?"

"Not quite. I'm in training."

"Yeah." He grabbed a glass from the collection on the kitchen table and went to pour himself some Sprite. "You gotta make all that noise this early in the morning?" he asked spitefully.

"I can work on something else for a little while, but I've got to get these cabinets down today."

Gulping down his soda, Eddie left the glass on the table. "Then do it, but I need some sleep." Without saying another word, Eddie got up and left the kitchen.

Neville closed up his tools and tried to think of what else he could work on for a while. He hoped that rude little runt wasn't going to be around every morning.

LeMar hadn't liked any of the carpet samples Rosie had shown him so far, so she asked him to meet her at another store. When she pulled up, she spotted LeMar's car right away. She took one quick look in the mirror before getting out of the car. Now instead of a few samples, he'd have hundreds from which to choose. He initially said he didn't know what he wanted, but now he had somewhat of an idea.

"See, I had something more like this in mind." He brushed past Rosie to point out a huge row of carpets that leaned against the wall.

Her body shivered as she looked at the carpet, then back at LeMar. "That's outdoor carpet. I don't think you want that on your living room floor."

He gave her a knowing nod. "You're right. That wouldn't look good in the living room, would it?"

"No, it wouldn't." She wanted to get this selection process over with as quickly as possible. This much time around LeMar was what she'd wanted to avoid. He made her nervous and jumpy.

She walked over to another row of samples and flipped through them. "Something like this is more of what I had in mind. It's durable, and it'll look great in your living—"

She stopped when she felt the heat from his breath on her neck. Glancing to her right, she looked at him. "Something wrong?"

"No." He smiled down at her, then touched the carpet. "Yeah, this is nice."

His hand rubbed across hers, and she felt a surge through her body. For just a second she had a mental picture of him naked and making love to her. She looked down at his hand, wanting to reach out and grip his long, strong fingers.

She cleared her throat and shook the visual out of her head. *What the hell is coming over me?* She'd known this would happen. She had to get away from him. Crossing her arms, she narrowed her eyes. "LeMar, why are we here?"

He turned and gave her a questioning look. "What do you mean? To find me some carpet."

"You know what I mean. I've shown you some beautiful samples. If I didn't know any better I'd say you were stalling and trying to waste my time."

He suppressed a smile as he walked away from her toward another row of carpet samples. "No. You've got it all wrong. I just want to find some durable carpet that also looks good. Since you're my designer, you have to take my hand and help me make a selection."

"Well, how are we doing, folks?" The salesman approached them.

"Just fine, he's narrowing his selection now." Rosie smiled up at LeMar. "Aren't you?"

He locked eyes with her. "Yes, I am. And I think I've found something I really like."

Her face flushed. Turning away, she walked over to a section of samples they'd discussed earlier. "Isn't this the one you said you liked?"

LeMar and the salesman followed her.

"That's a wonderful selection. A top-quality carpet. You can't go wrong with anything in this line." The salesman flipped through the samples, displaying them.

"It's very versatile also. This one would be good in the living room, or family room. Do you have any little ones?" He addressed them.

Rosie looked from the salesman to LeMar, then back at the salesman. "Oh, we're not married. We don't have any—I mean, I'm his designer. The carpet's for him." She pointed to LeMar.

LeMar moved next to her. "No, I'm afraid I'm not the lucky guy. But we do make a nice couple, don't you think?" He smiled at the salesman, who laughed along with him.

"I'm sorry. The way you two were getting along I just thought you were married. Then you must be pretty good friends?"

"You could say that," LeMar responded.

"I'm helping him select some carpeting." She looked up at LeMar. "Didn't you say you liked this one?" She pointed to a sample that was much like one she'd selected for him before.

"If you think it'll work, I guess it's the right one." He nodded his approval.

"Great, just let me know how much you need."

Rosie pulled a piece of paper from her purse. "I've got all the dimensions here." She handed the paper to the salesman.

"Let me check on something. I'll be right back." He walked away.

LeMar stepped back and grinned down at Rosie, then held out his hand. "Nice job."

She shook his hand, smiling. "Thank you. I thought you could use a little help making up your mind."

"Thanks, Mrs. Reed. Are you this bossy at home?"

She smiled and rolled her eyes at him. *Mrs. Reed.*

It has a nice ring to it. "I'm not bossy. I was helping you, that's all."

"Oh, so that's what you call it. Do you *help* your husband like that?"

She fished through her purse for a business card. Then she looked up at LeMar. "What I do at home is none of your business." She walked away in a casual manner and made her way to the counter to meet the salesman. After handing him her business card, they discussed the details of getting the carpet to Le-Mar's house. Then she caught up with LeMar.

"Everything's taken care of."

"Thank you. So what does Mr. Wright do?" LeMar asked.

Rosie didn't look at him. She reached in her purse and pulled out her cellular phone. "He's in computers, why?"

"I'm curious. I want to know what kind of man you married."

She dialed the office, but got a busy signal. "Why LeMar? Why do you care?" Unfortunately, Doreece wouldn't be able to rescue her from this conversation.

"I want to know if you're happy. Does he treat you well?"

She started out of the store, and he followed. "Yes, everything is fine. Do you have time this afternoon to look at some paint?"

He laughed as he opened the door for her to exit. "You know, I like how you change the subject every time I ask you a question you don't want to answer."

"I don't do that."

"Yes, you do. But it's cool. I shouldn't be meddling in your personal business anyway." He looked at his watch. "Thanks for helping me with the carpet. I've got a meeting at one o'clock so, I need to head back to work. Maybe I can meet you back at the house this evening to look them over?"

She sighed. "I hadn't planned on stopping by there today."

"I thought the landscapers were starting today?"

"They are, but Neville's taking care of everything. I don't need to be there."

"Oh, that should be interesting. He's at the house now with Eddie?"

"Neville is more than qualified to do the job."

"That's not what I'm worried about. Never mind. Look, we'll have to select those paint samples another day. Maybe you can bring some by tomorrow afternoon?"

"That'll be fine. I'll narrow it down to a select few." She turned away and said barely above a whisper, "Maybe that won't be as painful."

"I heard that." He smiled at her.

"I'm kidding." She noticed a sparkle in his hazel eyes that made her blush for a moment.

"Sure you were," he said sarcastically. Then he reached over to brush her cheek with the back of his hand.

She jerked away from his touch, then felt silly when she realized he was only wiping something off her face.

"You had a little carpet fuzz on your cheek, that's all. I wasn't trying to do anything."

"I'm sorry. You startled me. I guess I'm a little jumpy today." She bit her bottom lip.

"Something I remember about you is how you used to bite your lip whenever you were nervous." His voice lowered to a more husky, seductive tone. "Am I making you nervous?"

She tried to ignore it. "No, of course not. It's just a bad habit. It has nothing to do with you."

"Of course not. Why would I make you nervous—right?"

"Right. Why would you?"

"Sorry. My bad."

"I've changed a lot since college." Standing outside the carpet store, she didn't want to start going down memory lane.

"I don't think you've changed all that much. You still bite your lip, and you still blush whenever I smile at you." He tilted his head and smiled. "You see, I haven't forgotten."

"Well, too bad I can't say the same about you." She turned to her car. "I'm sure you've got to get to your meeting, and I've got to be running also."

"As always, it's been a pleasure."

A small dark car moved slowly down LeMar's street. It turned into the driveway and pulled all the way into the backyard. Two men got out and hurried up the steps. Shining a flashlight through the back window, the burglars could see that everything looked nice and quiet. Within a matter of seconds, one smashed the glass with his flashlight and stuck his hand inside to open the door.

No pets, no alarm. He was in the clear. His partner walked in behind him and they quickly started searching all the rooms.

They turned the bedrooms upside down. With their flashlights, they checked every drawer, under the beds, even inside the pillowcases. After about fifteen minutes, they gave up. What they wanted wasn't in the house.

Frustrated, they helped themselves to a few of Le-Mar's possessions.

Eight

Arriving home, LeMar stopped to grab his mail before going inside. As he walked through the door, he scanned the bills and advertisements.

A couple of CD cases lying in the middle of the floor caught his attention.

"What the hell!" He laid the bills on the foyer table and walked over to pick up the CDs. A stream of light came from the den. He slowly walked into the den. The first thing he noticed was the blank space above the television where his VCR used to sit. The prickly hairs on the back of his neck stood at attention. He'd been burglarized.

Throwing the CDs on the couch, he quickly ran through all the rooms downstairs. His CD player, along with his new DVD system, was also gone. He slammed his fist against the wall and stormed into the kitchen. The glass on the floor told the story of how someone got in.

He ran out of the kitchen and down the hall, then up the stairs two at a time. The way all the doors were ajar, he knew to expect the worse. He slowly opened the door to his office. His desk was naked without his computer.

"Damn it!" He walked over and grabbed his cordless phone, then dialed 911.

* * *

Two young police officers walked through LeMar's house, noting everything that was missing.

"Well, it looks like they came in through the back door in the kitchen. Just busted the glass and helped themselves. You ever think about getting an alarm system?" the younger cop with a severe case of acne asked.

LeMar hated smart-aleck police officers. "Yes, of course I've thought about it, but I just moved in and haven't had time to look into it yet."

The cop turned his back and started down the hall. "I'd look into that before moving any of my stuff in here. Atlanta's a nice place, but we do have crime, you know. You're in the big city now."

LeMar stood outside the den wanting to tell him he'd moved here from D.C., but he figured he shouldn't bother. If this cop thought LeMar was some country fool, so what?

The second cop came downstairs after inspecting the rooms upstairs. "You live here alone?" He directed his question to LeMar as he descended the stairs.

"A buddy of mine is staying with me for a little while."

"Does this buddy have any enemies?" He reached the bottom step and walked around his partner, over to LeMar.

LeMar shrugged. "Not that I know of, but I don't know everybody he knows. Why do you ask?"

"Because whoever broke in here was looking for something. The search was conducted with a purpose. Teenagers usually don't take the time to rip up the carpet, or rip open the pillows. They would have just taken the electronic equipment and left. Got any idea what they were looking for?"

"I don't have a clue." LeMar crossed his arms and leaned against the door frame.

"What does your friend do for a living?" the same officer asked, stroking his chin.

"Right now he's unemployed." LeMar realized what the officer was getting at. "I can't believe he had anything to do with this. I've known him since college. We're tight. Now, there's a guy here who's working with my designer, and some contractors doing landscaping that I don't know. It could have been one of them."

"Well, if you can get me some names and numbers, we'll check them out."

The officer that turned away from LeMar a minute ago walked back up and handed him a business card. "If you notice anything else missing, give us a call. Or if you think you know who did it, let us know. Now, the chances of you getting your belongings back aren't very good. You do know that, don't you?"

"I know it now," was all LeMar could say. At least he'd purchased homeowners' insurance.

After the officers left, LeMar sat in his office and stared at the spot where his computer used to be. He was pissed. He grabbed a sheet of paper from his desk and made a list of everyone who'd been in his house recently. The very first person to come to mind was Eddie's suspicious-looking friend. He didn't remember the guy's name. He'd have to question Eddie about his friend as soon as he saw him.

Or then again, it could have been Rosie's guy, Neville. He'd spent a lot of time in the house recently. LeMar reached over and picked up the phone. He already had Rosie's office number on speed dial. Her answering machine picked up, and he suddenly remembered how late it was. He'd been so upset he hadn't even checked the time. Her office had closed hours ago.

He went downstairs and found her business card with her home number written on the back. After the phone started ringing, he hoped it wasn't too unprofessional of him to call so late. Most of all, he hoped her husband wouldn't get upset.

"Hello." Rosie held her cell phone between her ear and shoulder.

"Rosie, it's LeMar. I hope I'm not calling too late. Did I disturb you?"

Stunned to hear his voice, she looked over at Carrie in the passenger seat. "I'm actually in my car right now. What can I do for you?"

"I had a break-in tonight."

Her eyes widened in horror. "You're kidding. What happened?"

"Somebody smashed the glass on the back door and stole a lot of my electronic equipment. I've been thinking about everybody who's been in this house recently. That's why I called you. I want to ask you about Neville."

"Oh, LeMar, Neville would never do something like that. I can vouch for him, trust me."

"Then how about those contractors who've been here? Do you have a phone number for the company?"

"Sure, but I can't get to it right now. I can't believe they'd do anything like that, either. I've worked with that company for years without one incident. I just can't believe it's any of my people."

"I don't know who did it. The police seemed to think they were looking for something. I have to check out everybody who's been in this house. I hope to at least get my computer back."

"I'm sorry, and I hope you find everything. But you can forget about Neville being involved in any way. How about your houseguest? Did you question him?" As far as she was concerned, that was the first place he should have gone.

"Not yet. But I plan to." In the back of his mind he had a nagging feeling that he didn't want to admit to.

"Did I catch you at a bad time?" he asked.

"I just picked up my neighbor, and I'm taking her home. But if you'll call me in the office tomorrow morning I'll give you my contractor's phone number. Neville and I plan on working on your house in the morning. So if you don't catch me early, I'll just leave the number on the kitchen table for you."

"No, why don't you call me at the office and leave it with Brenda, my secretary? That's if I don't catch you before you leave in the morning."

"Okay, sure. I'm real sorry about the house."

"Thanks, I'll catch you."

She hung up and shook her head. "Man, somebody broke into LeMar's house."

"Oh no, what happened, honey?" Carrie and Rosie were on their way home after Rosie had picked her up from visiting one of her friends at the senior citizen community.

"I'll find out all the details tomorrow, but he was burglarized. He called me to ask about Neville. I know Neville wouldn't do that. It's probably that low-life friend of his. I used to tell LeMar that that guy was no good. Looks like now he gets to find out for himself."

"How long have they been friends?" Carrie asked.

"Since college. They met freshman year and became big buddies. LeMar is more like a big brother to him, I think."

"Did he know David in school?"

Rosie hesitated before answering. She wasn't sure how much she wanted to tell Carrie about LeMar. After all, she was David's aunt, and she didn't know anything about Rosie's previous relationship with LeMar.

"I don't think they knew each other. I know David didn't pledge a fraternity, and LeMar hung out with the Omegas when he wasn't with Eddie."

"I talked with David a few weeks ago, did I tell you?"

"No, you didn't. How's he doing?" Rosie didn't have any hard feelings toward her ex-husband. She hadn't shared with Carrie the real reason for her divorce, only that David hadn't been faithful. However, Rosie and David knew the real deal.

"Oh, he's just fine. He might be down in a few weeks with his—oh, never mind. I haven't seen my baby since Christmas."

Carrie had been about to tell some of David's business, but had stopped. Rosie laughed to herself. David was her past, and she didn't care what he was doing. One thing she didn't believe in was traveling back in time. Because he'd tried to help her out in her time of need, she hoped he'd found happiness, but that's about as far as she went. LeMar, however, was another story. She'd wished he would be given a just reward for what he'd done to her.

"It's good to know he's doing well."

"I wish you two could have worked things out. I think you make such a lovely couple."

"David can be such a sweetheart, but we just weren't meant to be." She looked over at her neighbor sadly. "I'm sorry."

Carrie gave her a don't-you-never-mind wave.

"Honey, don't apologize to me. That's his loss. I didn't lose you." She laughed at her own cleverness.

"You sure didn't. I don't know what I'd do without you."

"Honey, that's the other way around. You are my lifesaver."

"Let's just say you're the best thing that came out of that marriage." Rosie meant that in more than one way.

"Too bad you two didn't have any children."

Rosie glanced out her side window. "Yeah, I guess."

If she hadn't miscarried, she wondered if David would have remained faithful to her, or would he have eventually strayed. Maybe they would have divorced with or without the child. And what would have happened once LeMar moved back into town?

LeMar was in the kitchen sweeping up glass when he heard the front door open. He waited for Eddie to step into the kitchen. He could hear him commenting on something before he walked in.

"Hey, what happened?" he asked, looking around with wild eyes.

"Somebody broke in."

"You kidding! What'd they take?"

"The VCR, DVD system, even my computer. Stuff that's probably been sold already. The police seemed to think they were searching for something."

"Like what?" Eddie asked.

"I was hoping you could tell me." LeMar dumped the glass into the garbage can, then looked up at Eddie.

Eddie's eyes widened with incredulity. "How am I supposed to know? You mean you think I had something to do with this?"

"Man, all I know is you come in here with some shady-looking guy, and a couple of days later my house gets broken into."

"Dru? Man, he don't do break-ins. You think I'd bring him in here if I thought he was a thief?"

"How well do you know him?"

"He's cool, man, he's my partner."

LeMar walked over to the window. He had to figure out a way to tape it up for the night. "Man, I don't know. Maybe you've got something he wants?"

Eddie shook his head. "All I've got is a bag full of clothes."

"Well, let me know if you find anything missing, so I can let the police know."

Eddie left the kitchen, and LeMar asked himself if he believed him. Eddie was right about one thing; he didn't have anything there but some clothes.

"This happens to be one job that I don't like," Rosie told Neville as she peeled a sheet of wallpaper from the wall.

"It's not so bad. Let's just be glad those thieves didn't find or want the wallpaper."

"I'm sure those thugs don't want any wallpaper. You can't sell it on the street."

"You'd be surprised at what all moves on the streets today."

Rosie gave Neville a sarcastic look. "Are you kidding? They stole his stereo equipment, even his CDs. They don't want wallpaper."

"You're probably—" Neville stopped, then looked toward the kitchen door when he heard someone coming down the stairs.

Rosie turned and saw Neville's pale face and furrowed brow. "What's wrong?"

"You'll see."

Whistling came from the other side of the door. Rosie stared at the door, not knowing if LeMar was about to walk through. When the door opened, Eddie appeared.

"Do you guys have to start so freaking early every morning?" He changed his tone when he saw Rosie. "Well, if it isn't Rosie Wright herself. How you doing, baby?"

The term of endearment coming from him made her sick to her stomach. "I'm fine, thank you." Rosie and Neville returned to their work.

"You sure are." He walked past Neville, never looking in his direction.

Even at this hour of the morning, his cologne was way too strong. Rosie watched him as he walked through the kitchen, giving her a wicked grin. When he winked at her, she flinched. "We didn't wake you, did we?" she asked, trying to get him to think of something else.

"No, I was up."

She watched him walk around the kitchen, fixing himself a glass of water and trying to find something to eat. She wanted him to leave. They kept working, stripping sheet after sheet of wallpaper.

"Mind if I fix myself some breakfast?" he asked as he pulled the carton of eggs out of the refrigerator.

Neville just looked at Rosie.

"I wouldn't if I were you. We need to strip this whole room." She gestured vaguely around the room.

"I'll make it quick." He continued to prepare a skillet for his eggs and grabbed some bread for toast. "So, how long is it going to take you to finish this room?"

Why was he talking to her? She didn't want to talk

to him. "A couple of weeks. You'll probably be gone before we finish."

"What makes you think that?"

"LeMar said you were staying for a couple of weeks. And we'll be longer than a couple of weeks on the whole house." She fought to keep the joy from her voice.

He made a sucking noise as he scrambled his eggs. "I don't know. I might stick around a little while longer."

Neville dropped his roll of wallpaper.

"Besides, I think your boy here likes looking at me every morning. Ain't that right, buddy?" Eddie laughed as he turned off his eggs and slid them onto a plate.

Rosie stepped down off the ladder. This man was beyond crude and vulgar. He was scum. Neville stepped down beside her.

"Eddie, was that necessary?" she said, fuming.

"What? I was just having a little fun with your friend. You guys look like you're about to gang up on me." He popped bread in the toaster, walked over, and stepped out onto the back porch.

"One day that guy is going to go too far." Neville picked up the wallpaper and started over.

"Does he harass you all the time?"

"No. He made a few offbeat comments once before, but I can handle him."

"Neville, why didn't you tell me?"

He shrugged. "I don't know. It just didn't seem important at the time. Like you said, he won't be staying long."

"Yeah, but we don't have to put up with his smart ass in the meantime."

The back door opened and Eddie returned. The smell of cigarette smoke followed him. "Well, designers, I've got to run. It was great having breakfast with you guys." He picked up his plate.

Rosie stopped him. "Eddie, I think we need to have a quick talk. Can I speak with you in the dining room?"

"Yeah, come on." He led the way.

"Eddie, I know you're not comfortable around Neville, but he works for me, and he's going to be working on this house for the next couple of months. I'd appreciate it if you didn't make homophobic comments like that."

"Homophobic? You mean he's gay?" he said sarcastically. "I never would have guessed."

"Don't play games with me. I don't want to have to talk to LeMar about this."

He laughed and set his plate on the table. Shaking his head, he walked around Rosie and took a seat. "What's he supposed to do? He's not my daddy." He dismissed her and began eating.

"I don't have to finish the house under these conditions. I'm sure if I made it clear to him how your presence is jeopardizing this job, you'd have to find a new place to stay."

He shook his head and stared into his eggs while she talked. When she finished, he winked at her. "You know, I could have a talk with him myself." He rolled his eyes toward the ceiling. "About something that happened, oh, say, twelve years ago."

Rosie's body went stiff. She watched that same wicked grin creep back onto his face. "What are you talking about?"

"Your secret's safe with me, maybe. By the way, how's your husband doing?"

Her cell phone rang, interrupting them. She grabbed it from her hip, but she wasn't able to concentrate. She wanted to know what Eddie knew. Did he know about the baby? Did he know that she was divorced?

"Rosie, you've got to get over here." Doreece sounded hurried. "Jimmy is here, and he's agreed to paint the murals for free. But you've got to see this design. I don't know what to think. Can you get over here now?"

"Excuse me," Rosie said, stepping over to the other side of the room. "I can't make it right now. I'm working on Mr. Reed's house." She turned and looked at Eddie.

He had crossed his arms and was leaning back in his chair.

"Rosie, if he walks away from here, he won't be back. And I don't have to tell you how in demand he is. He doesn't need us."

She knew she had to get there. This was just what she needed, free work from a decorative painter. "Okay, I'll run by as soon as I finish up here."

"You don't understand. He's about to leave. You need to get over here *now.*"

Neville poked his head out of the kitchen door. "Rosie, can I steal you for a minute?"

"Doreece, I'm on my way. Don't let him leave." She hung up. "Neville, I'll be right there."

Eddie pushed his chair back and stood up. "I'll get out of your way and let you guys finish up in there since you've got to leave."

"Eddie, I want to know what you meant earlier." She stood with her hands on her hips. He was bluffing. She didn't believe he knew anything about her.

He walked over and placed his hand on her shoulder. "Don't worry about it, baby. I'm sure neither one of us will have a need to talk with LeMar. Now, let me get out of here."

He turned down the hall and went upstairs. Rosie

was left wondering if she should bring LeMar into the situation. She wanted to think that she could handle it herself. She walked into the kitchen to help Neville.

After she helped him make some decisions about the wallpaper, she broke the news to him.

"Neville, I'm sorry, I've got to leave. That was Doreece. The painter is at the Colony House and I need to talk with him before he leaves. He's going to do the work for free."

"That's great."

"Yeah, but I'm gonna have to leave you here if you don't mind."

"Don't worry about that guy. I can handle him. He's eaten his breakfast, so I won't have to worry about him again today. Go on and take care of your business. This is my job to run with, remember?"

"I know, I just didn't mean to subject you to this."

"Rosie, get out of here. I've got this guy."

"Okay, hit me on the cell phone if you need me."

"I won't need you."

Nine

"I didn't want to tell you this over the phone, but Jimmy wants to paint this spiritual mural of naked women."

Rosie looked at Doreece as if she had two heads. "Doesn't he know it's for a child's room?"

"I told him. He says they're little angels and not naked women. But, Rosie, they've got breasts and everything."

Rosie shook her head, smiling at Doreece.

"Yep, you heard me right. Little breasts and, oh, I almost forgot. One is looking over her shoulder and she has a huge butt. I'm talking he painted a butt crack and everything. Girl, it's like those black velvet paintings from way back."

Unable to control herself, Rosie burst out laughing, and Doreece joined her. "Where is he now?" Rosie asked, setting her purse down.

"He's out doing something in his van. He parked out back."

Rosie started for the living room, then stopped and looked back at Doreece. "Naked angels for a child's room, go figure. I asked for something playful and whimsical."

Doreece shrugged. "I guess naked women are whimsical."

"Lord, those poor children would be frightened to death. I can see them now, lying there every night staring at the naked women on their walls, wondering how come the angels have bigger boobs than they do."

"See why I had to call you? He's ready to start painting now. I couldn't talk him out of it. But I know he'll listen to you."

"He's got no choice. It's my way or no way. And I don't care if he is doing it for free." With that said, she left the room and went searching for Jimmy.

After Rosie left, Neville tried his best to hurry with the kitchen. He didn't want to have to deal with Eddie again. He never had a problem when LeMar would pop in early. He was always such a gentleman. Too bad Neville couldn't say the same for his houseguest. LeMar always appeared so disappointed that Rosie wasn't there. Eddie, however, smelled as if he'd bathed in a whole bottle of cheap cologne and slept in his clothes all night. He reeked and cut off the circulation in the room. Something about him scared Neville. He looked like a cutthroat kind of guy. Like he might get into a fight and pull a knife. Neville wanted to stay out of his way.

No sooner had the thought crossed his mind than he heard whistling coming from the dining room. He prayed it was LeMar, but knew better.

Eddie walked in with his breakfast plate and stared at Neville. "Damn, you still here?"

"Afraid so." He tried to sound cheerful without looking around to see what type of expression was on Eddie's face. He heard the refrigerator door slam shut, and wondered if this guy was paying for all the food he kept eating. It seemed like every time he worked in the kitchen, Eddie came in to get something to eat.

"Say, I thought Rosie was the decorator? Why isn't she here every day instead of you?" Eddie asked gruffly.

The veins in Neville's neck stood out as he gritted his teeth. He counted to three before he responded. "I'm her assistant, and this job was assigned to me. If you have a problem with that, maybe you need to speak to her."

"I already did. I just don't like being at home all day with no queer."

"Who you calling a queer?"

"Is anybody else in the room? I'm certainly not talking to myself."

"Well, if you had a job like most people and didn't sit around the house all damned day, you wouldn't have to be here." Neville lost control. He tried to stop himself, but couldn't.

"Besides, I bet this man doesn't know you're laying up eating his food all day. You don't even wake up until almost noon. And you smell like—"

"Get out of here." Eddie stormed toward Neville, looking as if he wanted to strangle him. "Now! Get out!"

"I'm not the one who should be leaving—you should." Neville crossed his arms and stood his ground.

"Maybe you didn't hear me. I bet you'll hear this." Eddie drew back his arm and lunged forward as Neville let out a loud scream.

Rosie found Jimmy in the backyard with his van door wide open. A sheet lay on the ground where he prepared his paints. It was time for her to use her negotiating skills to get the right mural she wanted for the child's room.

"Jimmy, how you doing?" She greeted him with a gleeful smile.

He looked up. "Hey there, I'm fine. I didn't expect to see you here today."

"Doreece called me." She walked closer, and they exchanged a friendly hug. With his dreadlocks and his old baggy paint-splattered pants and boots, he had a real struggling-artist look.

"Uh-huh. That call wouldn't have had something to do with my angels, would it?"

"Yeah, I'm afraid it did. She expressed a little concern over your angels. Do you mind if I see the drawing?"

"Not at all." He reached in the van and grabbed a rolled-up piece of paper. "Let's go over to the hood of the truck." He wiped his hands off on his pants.

Rosie followed him to the front of his van. He unrolled the drawing and held down the edges. "I think these angels are perfect for a child's room."

She stared at the little, naked, fully developed sketches. The first thing she noticed was a nipple. Quickly, she pressed a finger against her top lip, stifling a laugh. *What in the hell is he thinking about?* She took a step back and crossed her arms.

"Jimmy, have you painted anything for a child's room before?"

He let go of the paper and it rolled back up. "No, but you've seen my portfolio and some of the work I've done before. What's the problem?"

She unrolled the paper and pointed to the nipples. "This is the problem. We're preparing this room for two little girls barely ten years old. I had something more playful and childlike in mind."

"But these angels are playful." He looked down at the drawing.

"Jimmy, look. Unless you can tone this down, I'm afraid I can't use the mural. No nipples."

An approaching car caught Rosie's attention. She looked around the van at the Lexus pulling up. She didn't recognize the driver. Then, a tall handsome movie-star-looking brother stepped out of the car. Simultaneously, Doreece walked out of the patio door with a sneaky smile on her face. He removed his sunglasses when Doreece walked up to shake his hand. *Who is that?* Rosie wondered. It definitely wasn't missing in action Tony.

"I guess I could make a few adjustments." Jimmy scratched at his beard as he ran his hand across his drawing.

Rosie turned her attention back to him. "Please do. Jimmy, I really appreciate your donation and all. It just needs some tweaking."

"I guess I could adjust a few body parts."

"How about real angelic figures without the breasts or such defined bodies?" She couldn't help but laugh now. "Honey, we'd scare those little girls to death."

He laughed a little with her. "Yeah, I guess. But you know these angels will blend in with anything and not take away from the room at all. Do you feel where I'm coming from?"

"Yes, I do." Rosie's thoughts trailed away from him as she frowned at Doreece and the man coming toward her. She couldn't afford to pay anyone else to do anything.

"Rosie, I'd like you to meet Phillip Hamilton." Doreece stood there with a broad grin on her face as Phillip extended his hand to Rosie.

"Hello." She shook his hand, slightly embarrassed

because she didn't remember who he was. Should she know him?

"It's nice to meet you. Your sister's told me a lot about you and your project."

"Phillip's interested in being a sponsor. Remember me telling you about him?" Doreece winked at Rosie.

"Oh, yes, I remember." Doreece had said he would call. "Come on, let's go inside and talk." She gave a few last-minute instructions to Jimmy before Doreece and Phillip followed her inside the house.

Phillip had smooth, dark, and delicious Hollywood-looking skin. He reminded her of Morris Chestnut, from the movie *The Best Man*. His outfit was casual, but it looked expensive. Where on earth did Doreece meet him?

Before Rosie opened her mouth, Doreece excused herself and left the two of them alone in the kitchen. A small glass-top dinette set sat by the bay window. "Won't you have a seat?" Rosie offered.

"Thank you. Doreece tells me you need another sponsor to help furnish the house?"

"And she tells me that someone is you." He made the dinette set look like kid's furniture. He flashed her a thousand-dollar smile with a beautiful set of teeth. She could smell his cologne dancing beautifully about the room.

"It might be. I'm looking for a community project to get involved with. And I like the idea of making home ownership possible for a single mother and her daughters. I'd like to do whatever I can to be involved."

She couldn't believe her ears. She'd been scratching for sponsors for months and this man just walked in, the answer to her prayers. She wanted to jump across the table and kiss him, but settled for offering a handshake.

"Well, Mr. Hamilton—"

"Call me Phillip."

She blushed and bit her lip to keep from grinning like a simple schoolgirl. "Okay, Phillip. How'd you like to take a walk around the house? I can tell you a little about the family we're moving in and anything else you'd like to know."

"Thank you, I'd like that."

She gave him the grand tour, stopping to point out what had been purchased with sponsorship help so far. She put extra emphasis on how bad things would look if she weren't able to complete the house this year. Phillip followed her, showing great interest. He told her several times how he admired women who thought of more than themselves and took the time to give back to their community. He also mentioned his church a couple of times, and how he worked with church projects.

After the tour, they sat down at the kitchen table again to talk money. They agreed on an amount, and he asked to be informed on the progress. He also expressed an interest in being at the open house ceremony.

"Phillip, I really appreciate this, and if you have any friends that would be interested in sponsorship this year or next year, let me know. You know, we have a lot of sports figures in this town, and I've never thought to ask them for sponsorship."

"You should. A lot of us are involved in community work. I usually participate in about three projects a year."

"If you don't mind me asking, how did you and Doreece meet?"

"My sister introduced us. I think they go to the same hairdresser, or they do something in the same salon." He chuckled. "She told me about the project and showed me a brochure about Yahimba Designs. I told myself, *This is something you need to check out.*"

"And I'm glad you did."

"So am I. Before I write you a check, I need to speak with my accountant. I'm sure it won't be a problem, I just clear everything with him before making any business investments."

"Sure, I understand."

"You know, we just met, and other than what I read in the brochure, I don't know much about you. We need a chance to get acquainted. Week after next a partner of mine is having an art showing at this gallery downtown. There's a cocktail hour where lots of celebrities will be. How'd you like to join me?"

She blinked fast twice. "Me?" she asked, holding a hand to her chest.

"Yes, if you're not busy Thursday after next? It would be a great networking opportunity for you, and a great time for me to learn more about the scope of the project."

Was he asking her out in a sly way? It sounded like a date; then it sounded like a business opportunity she couldn't afford to miss. What did she have to lose? Nothing.

"Sure, I'm game."

"Great, then it's a date. I'll pick you up around seven-thirty. It's at the Kiang Gallery of Contemporary Art downtown."

"Okay, seven-thirty's good." Maybe it was a real date.

This time, when she shook his hand, she thought she'd never seen a man with such nicely manicured fingers. Had he actually played ball? Didn't ballplayers have rough callused hands? She had a date with a retired ballplayer, and found herself wishing she knew more about sports.

***

For girls' night out, Rosie, Sharon, and another old friend of theirs, Eliz, met at Café 290. They hadn't been to that particular club in more than a year. Rosie loved the live jazz band, while Sharon favored all the available men around the bar. Married with two children, Eliz just loved getting out with her single friends every once in a while.

After Sharon entertained them with stories of her last date with a masseur, Rosie told them about Phillip Hamilton.

"Yes, I remember him. Girl, I loved to watch him play," Sharon said enthusiastically.

"So did I," Eliz added.

"I didn't know he lived here. That brother is beyond fine. I've never heard any wild stories about him and drugs, or anything else," Sharon added.

"Rosie, sounds like you've got yourself a good catch," Eliz offered.

"It's just a networking function, not really a date. I'm not looking for anyone right now anyway."

"You mean to tell me that if the perfect man walked into your life right now, you'd turn him down?" Sharon gave Rosie a skeptical look. "Tell the truth now. If you can't be honest with us, who can you be honest with?"

Rosie stirred her drink, absently looking down into it. She couldn't help but smile. "Well, I'm no fool. Then again, there's no such thing as a perfect man. So that won't be happening in my lifetime."

"I don't know now. That guy we saw a couple of weeks ago, your old school friend, he looked damned near perfect to me." Sharon turned to Eliz and gave her a quick description of LeMar.

"Looks can be deceiving. Trust me, he's far from perfect," Rosie explained.

"So was this guy an old love?" Eliz asked Rosie.

"We're old college friends, that's all."

"Did I know him?" Eliz asked.

"No, I met him at Clark the first time I went to school, not when you and I were there."

"Eliz, you should see this guy. I mean, he's fine. The girl didn't even want to introduce me. He had to introduce himself."

"I did introduce you!" Rosie said, shocked.

"After he asked who I was." Sharon leaned back, crossing her arms. "What's up with that? Girl, you know I'm in the market."

"I told you I was surprised to see him. I just forgot." Rosie had a thought. She may have figured out a way to get rid of LeMar and shut Sharon up.

"Ladies, ladies, what's up?"

Rosie looked up from the bar to see Eddie standing with his arms wide open, smiling like a Cheshire cat. He looked Eliz up and down, checking her out. She was the only one he didn't know.

Eliz returned his stare, and no one said a word.

"Come on, ladies, give me some love." He put his arms down and squeezed between Rosie and Eliz at the bar. "And who is this lovely young lady?"

"Mrs. Mullins is the name." Eliz held out her hand.

Eddie shook her hand and turned to Rosie when he heard her talking to Sharon.

"I knew something about this place had changed. The clientele's gone down." Sharon took another sip of her drink.

"I see what you mean." Rosie turned back to Eddie.

He leaned forward, resting his elbows on the bar. "If it isn't Sharon, the man-eater."

Rosie didn't laugh, and Sharon rolled her eyes at him. "Eddie, go slide back under your rock, why don't you."

He flinched and winked at her.

The band stopped playing and tables were cleared from the dance floor. The DJ came on, so the crowd hit the floor. Eliz was the first one asked to dance. Sharon turned around to face the dance floor. Rosie tried to turn away from Eddie, but he wouldn't budge.

"Can I buy you a drink?" he asked Rosie as he took Eliz's seat.

"No, thank you, I'm not finished with this one."

Two men walked through the club dressed like pimps from a video—complete with gold chains and hats. Rosie knew a gangster when she saw one. She shook her head, thinking how only young professionals used to crowd the place. Now, the professionals and the pimps mingled in the same crowd.

One of the men walked over and stood next to Eddie. They shook hands, and he leaned over and said something to Eddie. Rosie wanted to get up and move away, but he looked around Eddie and gave her a nasty smile. She knew they were up to something underhanded. That guy was trouble on two legs.

Someone asked Sharon to dance just as the guy walked away. That left Rosie and Eddie together. She tried to lean away from him so people wouldn't think they were together. However, it didn't work. A few men glanced from her to Eddie, but none asked her to dance.

She could feel Eddie staring at her, and she wanted

to scream. "So, where's your buddy at tonight?" she finally asked.

"I wondered how long it would be before you got around to asking me about him. He didn't want to come out."

He probably couldn't stand the company, she thought. She nodded her head, then turned to face the bar, not wanting anyone to see her talking to him.

Eddie turned around also and leaned closer to her. "Let me ask you something?" He didn't wait for her to respond. "Why do you give me such a hard time? We used to get along."

She sat straight up with a shocked look on her face. "We did? When?"

"Before I introduced you to LeMar. Did you forget that's how you guys met?"

She remembered Eddie had tried to rap to her, then he'd introduced her to his friend and she'd been in love. She'd wanted LeMar the day she laid eyes on him. The one thing she didn't remember was ever being friends with Eddie. He'd gotten on her nerves from the first day she met him.

"No, I remember how we met. But I don't ever remember us being big buddies or anything." She pointed from him to her.

"I shouldn't have ever introduced you guys. I should have kept you for myself." He motioned for the bartender to bring him another drink.

"Ready for that drink now?" He turned back to Rosie.

She had a dumbfounded look on her face. Her mind was still trying to register what he'd said a few seconds ago. She didn't know whether to laugh or get upset. He was out of his mind. "No, I'm fine." Instead of responding, she just shook her head and laughed to herself.

Spinning around on her stool, Rosie faced the dance floor and wished her girlfriends would come back. They didn't have to dance to every record. She could see Sharon through the crowd grinning at her.

"So, why don't we get out of here?" Eddie whispered in Rosie's ear.

She sneered at him, watching him out of the corner of her eye. She felt the steam rolling from her ears and nose. Her eyes narrowed as she recoiled in horror. She couldn't take the smell of him.

"If you don't get up from that seat and leave me the hell alone . . . Eddie, I am not going anywhere with you." Her voice rose, then she rolled her eyes at him.

"Come on. Your husband doesn't have to know."

She stood from her stool. "Okay, if you won't leave, I will."

He grabbed her by the arm. "Rosie, I'm sorry. I was just joking with you. Lighten up, girl." He topped it off with a big smile.

Jerking her arm away, she spun around and wanted to swing at him. Control was hard to come by, but she mustered up enough to keep her hands to herself. "Eddie, I tried to be nice, but you're trying my patience. I have to be nice to LeMar, but I don't have to be nice to you. I'd appreciate it if—"

"Oh, you don't have to be nice to LeMar," he interrupted. "At least not right now, while he's in the dark. But once he finds out, I suspect you'll want to be nice to him."

"When he finds out what?" she asked, nearly shouting.

"Hey, girl, what's going on? It's getting a little loud over here." Sharon walked up and put her hand on Rosie's shoulder.

"What are you talking about, Eddie?" Rosie didn't take her eyes off him.

"What?" He turned from Rosie to Sharon. "You looking awful fine, Ms. Sharon."

Sharon held up her open palm. "Don't even go there, Eddie. You know I don't like you, so get to stepping. You're blocking all the guys from checking us out." She waved her hand at him. "Scoot, scoot."

He raised his drink to Rosie, then walked away.

"Girl, I'm sorry I left you so long. What was he talking about anyway?"

Rosie's heart raced as he walked away. "I'm not sure."

Ten

Monday morning Neville called in sick, so Rosie had to meet the contractors at LeMar's house. For fear she'd have to deal with Eddie again, she rescheduled for later in the day. When she arrived around noon, she was elated to see that Eddie wasn't there. While the contractors worked in the kitchen, she went upstairs to hang curtains.

She turned up the radio while she worked since she had the house to herself. Walking around upstairs, she was reminded of how beautiful the house was. The guest bedrooms didn't need much work. She'd ordered new bedding for the rooms and did a little rearranging.

Every time she passed the room Eddie used, she could smell him. Until he moved out, she wasn't about to touch that room. His cheap cologne was so strong and overbearing she didn't know how LeMar could stand it. She sung along with the radio and went about her business of hanging curtains.

LeMar pulled up and noticed Rosie's car in the driveway. To what did he owe this honor? Maybe he needed to bring his reports home to work on them more often. He also noticed the contractors' truck parked in the backyard. So much for having her to himself, he thought. Downstairs, men were working in the kitchen, but there was no sign of Rosie. He carried his briefcase with him upstairs to his make-shift office. He heard the music coming down the hallway.

Rosie walked out of the spare bedroom and jumped when she saw LeMar standing in the hall.

"Oh, you scared the mess out of me," she said.

"I guess you couldn't hear me over the radio," he remarked.

"Sorry." She walked into his office and turned the volume down. He followed her.

"No problem. I'm just surprised to find you working here today. I usually run into Neville." He set his briefcase on the desk and took off his jacket.

"He's a little under the weather, so I thought I'd come by and do a few things. Besides, I had to let the contractors in."

He just looked at her as they stood there in silence for a few minutes.

"Well, I'd better get out of here and let you get to work. Looks like you're bringing work home with you." She walked toward the door.

He looked over at his briefcase. "Yeah, I've got this report that I couldn't really concentrate on at work. Thought I'd bring it home and knock it out. But you don't have to run off. Continue doing whatever you were doing. I promise I won't get in your way." He loosened his necktie and pulled it off.

The room appeared to be shrinking, or was it her imagination? "I'm just about finished anyway." She turned again to leave.

"Let me see what you've done." He followed her out of the office and across the hall into the guest room.

"Hey, this works well. I like the way the curtains match the bedspread. And I guess all those pillows are cool, too." He walked around the room, noticing all the changes she'd made.

"I'm glad you like it. This weekend I've got a few more things coming in for the other bedroom. After the bathrooms and your bedroom, we'll be ready to move your office downstairs."

"Great." He sat down on the four-poster bed and bounced as if he were testing it out.

He managed to make her uncomfortable no matter where they were. She picked up her bag of curtains and headed for the door.

"Speaking of the weekend, what's going on? I don't go out much, but I thought I'd hang out for a little this weekend."

"I don't know. Do you listen to V-104? They always let you know about the parties going on around town."

"No, I don't listen to the radio very much, I'm afraid."

She had plans Saturday night with Sharon, but didn't know if he would be interested. "You know, this club I belong to is having a dance Saturday night at 201 Courtland. It should be very nice. Why don't you meet us there?"

"Who's us? You and your husband?" He wanted to meet her husband, but he didn't particularly want to party with them.

"No, me and a girlfriend. It starts around eight o'clock. I hope you can join us."

"Sounds like a plan. Looks like I've got my first date."

Rosie and Sharon arrived at the club a few minutes after eight. They couldn't be late because Rosie had a big surprise in store for Sharon. And it was important that they had a table. If they wound up standing around the bar, her plan wouldn't work. Luckily, most of the African Grapevine members hadn't arrived yet. They got a nice table for four and piled their purses in one chair.

After ordering drinks, they mingled a bit. Rosie kept glancing at her watch, wondering if LeMar was going to show up. She just hoped he wouldn't bring Eddie with him.

Several men dropped by the table, and Sharon enjoyed flirting with them. Rosie just watched and laughed. Minutes later, she looked up and saw LeMar making his way across the room. Momentarily, she was taken aback by how handsome and sexy he looked. Heads in the room turned as he passed. Women were checking him out, and she knew he had to be aware of it. However, he'd never been vain, nor thought he was God's gift to women.

Sharon's male friends had left the table before LeMar approached.

"Hello. I bet you didn't think I was going to show," he said to Rosie as he pulled out the extra chair next to Sharon.

Rosie smiled at him and observed the stunned look on Sharon's face. "I figured you were just running late."

He sat down and looked at Sharon. "Hi, I remember you." Then he glanced at Rosie.

"Yes, you two met before. Sharon, LeMar. LeMar, Sharon." She introduced them again.

Sharon set her drink down and wiped off her hand before shaking his. "Yes, I remember you, too. You're Rosie's friend from college."

"I'm her client now."

Rosie tried not to smile so much that they would

know they were being set up. She moved closer to Sharon to talk, and left the chair holding the purses as a divider between her and LeMar. "Sharon, you should see his house. It's wonderful."

"It will be after you finish." He motioned for a waiter to come over.

"Would either of you like another drink?"

"One's my limit tonight, I'm driving, thank you," Rosie said.

"I'll have another glass of white wine, thank you." Sharon finished off the sip of wine remaining in her second glass.

Rosie tried to get them engaged in a conversation, which was fairly easy. Once they seemed to be getting along, she decided to make her exit. Sharon wouldn't be going anywhere now that she had a drink on the way. Neither of them would.

"Will you two excuse me? I see a friend that I've been trying to catch up with for weeks. I'll be back in a few minutes." LeMar stood as she stood. "You don't have to do that. Sit down and enjoy yourself." She took her drink and walked away. The look on their faces was priceless.

She made it her business to stay away for at least thirty minutes. When she saw Sharon going into the ladies' room, she followed her.

"Girl, where have you been?" Sharon asked.

"Talking to Michael. I haven't seen him in months." Rosie lied.

"Honey, your friend is so fine."

"You like him?"

"What's not to like? He's got a beautiful smile, and I love a man with a sexy smile. And he's so intelligent. Just my kind of guy."

"Great."

Sharon turned and placed her hands on her hips.

"I smell a rat here. What the hell do you think you're doing?"

"Nothing. If you two hit it off, that's great. You said you'd date him if I wasn't interested."

"And you're not interested in him?"

Rosie cringed. "No way. But he's a good catch. Has he asked you out yet?"

"Not yet." She looked in the mirror and applied her lipstick. "But it's still early."

Rosie and Sharon returned to the table.

"We thought we'd lost you," LeMar said to Rosie as she sat down.

"I was just running my mouth." She tried to keep her conversation with LeMar to a minimum. Every time someone she knew passed the table, she stopped them and talked. She danced with friends and left Sharon to entertain LeMar.

LeMar sensed he was being bamboozled. Here he was hoping to spend some time with Rosie, and she made sure he spent most of the night with Sharon. Not that Sharon wasn't a beautiful woman. She just wasn't the woman for him. He wanted Rosie back.

"So how long did you say you've been in town?" Sharon asked.

"About a month now. I can't believe how the city has changed since I left."

"Yeah, Atlanta's ever changing, that's for sure. I've been here for more than ten years."

He wasn't sure how long he could keep up the small talk with Sharon. Maybe he'd just excuse himself and go home. As he listened to her talk, he realized he could turn this thing around on Rosie. Sharon was a nice, attractive woman. And she'd probably go out with him if he asked. That appeared to be what Rosie wanted, but did she really? Two could play at this little game.

Thursday evening rolled around faster than Rosie anticipated. She kept telling herself this was not a date, but a networking opportunity. She made sure she had plenty of business cards in her purse. Phillip picked her up on time and drove down to the gallery as fast as traffic would allow him. Their conversation consisted of more details about his community work. Once inside the gallery, Rosie was introduced to several celebrity sports figures. She talked up Yahimba Designs and her project as much as possible.

"Phillip, I want to thank you for inviting me tonight. I've had a wonderful time, and I've met so many people." The potential business in the room was phenomenal.

"I'm glad you're enjoying yourself. Did you let them know that I'm working on your project?"

"Oh, I may have told a few people." Was that so important?

"Cool. I just figured if you told them I was participating, they might want to help more." He looked at his watch. "Well, we've been here—what, about an hour and a half? Come on, let's get out of here."

Everything about this evening was too fast-paced for Rosie. Was that how the rich moved? They didn't really have time to do anything, so they popped in and out? He peeled away in the same fashion as when they arrived. She wanted to know what the hurry was.

"Your friend is a very good artist. I loved his work."

"Yeah, he's pretty good." He pulled the visor down and looked in the mirror, smoothing over his mustache. When he finished it, he smiled over at Rosie. "Let's stop by the Martini Club. I could use a drink."

Considering it was only nine-thirty and still early, she didn't mind stopping. "Sounds like a good idea."

What she didn't know was that a lot of his friends were waiting for him. What he didn't know was that she knew one of his friends.

"Rosie, it's good to see you."

Leonard Hunter, an attorney friend of hers, was also a friend of Phillip's. She welcomed the friendly face.

"Leonard, it's good to see you, too. How have you been?" She kissed him on the cheek.

"Wonderful. What you doing hanging out with this bum?" He slapped Phillip on the back.

"Don't listen to a word he says." Phillip hugged Leonard and shook his hand. They exchanged pleasantries before Phillip saw another good friend and went to greet him.

Rosie was left standing with Leonard.

"Like I said, what you doing with him?" This time he didn't have a smile on his face.

"He's a new sponsor for my Colony Homes project. He's donating some money to help furnish the house."

He nodded and snickered. "Some people think all you have to do is throw a little money at things, and they'll go away."

"What are you talking about?"

"Phillip got himself in a little bit of trouble, so his manager told him to go out and drum up some good publicity for himself. Guess that's where you come in."

She tried not to look as stunned as she felt. *This is only a business-type date anyway.* "So you don't think he's genuinely interested in the project?" *Not to mention me.*

"I doubt it, but don't tell him I told you so. Look

at this as an opportunity to get as much as you need for your project. Right now, he needs you just as much as you need him."

"Can I ask what he did?"

"You haven't heard it on the news?"

"I'm not really into sports."

"He was dating some college student. Got her pregnant and paid for the abortion. She says he promised to marry her if she got rid of the child. She was looking to sue him, but he somehow talked her out of it."

Her eyebrows shot up in surprise. Not him. Not the movie-star-looking, incredibly handsome, and sexy man with whom she was looking forward to working. "Wow, I'm stunned."

"So was everybody else. He denies it, of course. That's why I asked what you were doing with him."

"Leonard, I had no idea. We just left a gallery opening for one of his friends. He's introduced me to lots of people tonight."

"Oh, he's a good guy to know. He knows everybody in town. He's also a pretty generous guy. It's just that right now he's working on a little image repair, and I didn't want to see you get caught up into anything."

"Thanks a lot, I'll remember that."

"Hey, if you guys are finished gossiping about me, I've got somebody I want Rosie to meet." Phillip walked up behind Leonard.

"Trust me, we had better things to talk about." Leonard smiled at Rosie. "Take care if I don't see you again tonight."

She smiled at him conspiratorially. "I will, and thank you again." She walked off with Phillip, reassured that this evening was all about business.

***

A week after Rosie hooked up LeMar and Sharon, they had a date planned. Rosie would never admit it to anyone, but she was slightly jealous. What had seemed like a great idea one moment, didn't look so good now. What would she do if LeMar fell in love with Sharon and they ended up together? Could she handle that? Could their friendship handle it?

Neville was still sick, so Rosie found herself working at LeMar's house again. She had placed some African artifacts throughout the house. His guest rooms were complete. All but the room in which Eddie stayed.

"Hello, looks as if I got lucky again today," LeMar said as he walked in the front door. Rosie was in the foyer, positioning a lamp on the table.

She looked at her watch, pretending not to have realized the time. "Wow, what time is it?"

"Four-thirty," he answered, glancing at his own watch.

"I must have gotten caught up in my work today. I'd planned on leaving at four."

"Where's your helper?"

"He's feeling a little under the weather today."

"Man, good help is hard to find, isn't it?" He set his briefcase down and walked over to the table near her, dropping the mail onto it.

"Neville's usually very reliable. I don't understand. He must be real sick."

"Rosie, I wanted to thank you for inviting me to that party Saturday night. I had a good time."

"Great, I knew you would enjoy yourself." She wanted to ask him something about Sharon, but decided to wait and see if he offered the information.

"Well, mind if I take a look at what you've done so far?"

"Sure. The guest rooms are finished. Maybe you'd like to start up there."

"Okay, let's check it out." He started up the stairs and she followed.

"What's this?" He reached over and picked up a wood stick propped against the wall.

"African walking sticks. They're accent pieces. I've got to pick up the vase they go in."

"Nice." He nodded and continued up the steps.

He walked through the guest rooms, giving his nod of approval. "This looks great. It's like something out of a magazine."

"Thank you."

He went down the hall and pointed to Eddie's room. "What about that one?"

"As soon as he's gone, I can work in there."

"No problem. He'll be leaving in a few days anyway."

"That's good." She hadn't meant to say that out loud. What she really wanted to do was talk to LeMar about his association with Eddie. Trouble seemed to follow Eddie around, and if LeMar kept him too close, he'd soon be in trouble, too.

He let out a long sigh and shook his head. "I need to talk to him. Initially, it was a few days, then that turned into weeks. But I don't think his girl will let him back in."

"He has a girlfriend?"

LeMar laughed. "Is that so hard to believe?"

"Incredibly." Rosie laughed with him. "He just gets under my skin. I can't explain it."

"You have to understand he's had a hard life."

"There's no excuse for that man being as sleazy as he is. He's every woman's nightmare."

LeMar left the guest room and went into his room.

"Strong words." He looked back at her. "You really don't like the guy, do you?"

She shrugged. "He's your friend. Not mine." The suspense was killing her. Was he going to tell her about him and Sharon or not?

He looked around the room. "Wow, is this the same room?"

"I made a few adjustments today." She'd purchased a new bedspread set. Over the blinds she'd hung a rod and draped a bold window treatment that matched the bedding. He now had a pair of matching lamps instead of the mismatched ones he'd had before. In the corner was a big comfortable bedroom chair.

He walked around the room touching the curtains, the bedding, and even the lamp shades. "I'm pleased, Mrs. Wright."

That was the first time she'd heard him use her married name. Something about the way he looked at her had changed. He wasn't flirting with her the way he always did.

"Thank you. I'm glad you like it."

They left the rooms upstairs and went into the den. He wanted to look at the plans for the kitchen and see how things were coming along. "I'm concerned about the kitchen. Do you think you'll finish on time?"

"Yes. If Neville doesn't return in a day or two, I'll have my contractor finish up. Don't worry, it's not a problem."

They went over all the remaining details of the house and discussed the time line for finishing. The basement billiard room still had to be completed. He also wanted to make sure she didn't need any more money. At present she was coming in on budget.

"I'm not worried. I'm sure you'll take care of everything." He handed the plan back to her, reaching for her hand as he did. "Where's your wedding ring?"

She bolted straight up and stared at him. "It's at the jewelers being cleaned, why?"

"I was just wondering why you weren't wearing it," he said, shrugging.

"Well, now you know."

He sat back on the couch as she rolled up the kitchen plans and put them away. His behavior this evening was totally throwing her for a loop.

"If Neville's not feeling well, I may be back in the morning. Do you think Eddie will be here?"

He shook his head, then said, "I don't think so. I haven't seen him the last couple of days. There's no telling where he is."

She stood and headed for the front door. "Well, I've got to be running. I have an appointment across town at six-thirty."

He looked down at his watch. "Yeah, and I'd better start getting ready."

"Got a hot date tonight?" Since he wouldn't tell her, she'd pull it out of him.

"Didn't your friend tell you?"

"No, what?" She pretended not to know anything.

"I asked Sharon out. She was telling me about this restaurant with belly dancers called the Imperial Fuzz. I thought we'd try it out. Yeah," he said, looking down at his watch. "I've got a little more than an hour to get changed and pick her up."

He walked her to the door. Right now she was glad he couldn't see her face. She wanted to be happy for them. Why else had she tried to set them up? Sharon was his hot date, and Rosie knew just how hot that date could get. Why did they have to

3 QUICK STEPS
TO RECEIVE YOUR "THANK YOU" GIFT
FROM THE EDITOR

Send this card back and you'll receive 4 FREE Arabesque
novels! The introductory shipment of 4 Arabesque novels – a
$23.96 value – is yours absolutely FREE!

There's no catch. You're under no obligation to buy anything.
You'll receive your introductory shipment of 4 Arabesque
novels absolutely FREE (plus $1.50 to offset the costs of
shipping & handling). And you don't have to make any
minimum number of purchases—not even one!

We hope that after receiving your books you'll want to
remain an Arabesque subscriber. But the choice is yours to
continue or cancel, anytime at all! So why not take us up on
our invitation to receive 4 Arabesque Romance Novels, with
no risk of any kind. You'll be glad you did!

Call us
TOLL-FREE
at 1-888-345-BOOK

THE EDITOR'S "THANK YOU" GIFT INCLUDES:

- 4 books absolutely FREE (plus $1.50 for shipping and handling)
- A FREE newsletter, *Arabesque Romance News*, filled with author interviews, book previews, special offers, and more!
- No risks or obligations. You're free to cancel whenever you wish... with no questions asked.

BOOK CERTIFICATE

Yes! Please send me 4 FREE Arabesque novels (plus $1.50 for shipping & handling). I understand I am under no obligation to purchase any books, as explained on the back of this card.

Name _____

Address _____ Apt. _____

City _____ State _____ Zip _____

Telephone ( ) _____

Signature _____

Offer limited to one per household and not valid to current subscribers. All orders subject to approval. Terms, offer, & price subject to change. Offer valid only in the U.S.

Thank you!

AN091A

Accepting the four introductory books for FREE (plus $1.50 to offset the cost of shipping & handling) places you under no obligation to buy anything. You may keep the books and return the shipping statement marked "cancelled". If you do not cancel, about a month later we will send 4 additional Arabesque novels, and you will be billed the preferred subscriber's price of just $4.00 per title. That's $16.00 for all 4 books for a savings of 33% off the cover price (Plus $1.50 for shipping and handling). You may cancel at any time, but if you choose to continue, every month we'll send you 4 more books, which you may either purchase at the preferred discount price. . . or return to us and cancel your subscription.

THE ARABESQUE ROMANCE CLUB: HERE'S HOW IT WORKS

ARABESQUE ROMANCE BOOK CLUB
P.O. Box 5214
Clifton NJ 07015-5214

PLACE
STAMP
HERE

go watch some belly dancers? What happened to
boring movies?

"Well, enjoy yourself," she said, walking out.

"Oh, I plan to."

Eleven

Rosie paced around the living room, wanting to pick up the phone, then not wanting to pick up the phone. *What excuse can I use?* She was dying to know if LeMar had carried Sharon to a restaurant as intimate as the Imperial Fuzz. The suspense was killing her.

She didn't dare call for fear Sharon would think she was interested in LeMar, and she couldn't chance that. She'd have to hold out until the next day when Sharon would call to brag about it.

To keep her mind off things, she washed the dishes. The clock over the sink read six o'clock. Minutes later, she turned to wipe off the stove, and it was 6:05. In a little while they'd be going on their date. As she turned to walk out of the kitchen, her eyes travelled straight to the clock.

"This is ridiculous," she said aloud. She threw her tea towel on the counter and left the kitchen. She asked herself why she'd set them up in the first place. What had been on her mind?

Unable to take the pressure any longer, she went into her office and picked up the phone. Her mind raced and her heart beat so fast, she almost hung up. She listened as it rang. She had no idea what she'd say once he answered. If he answered.

She practiced her excuses for calling as she paced around her desk. After the fifth ring, she concluded he'd probably already left. She quickly slammed the phone down. *What was she doing?*

LeMar rubbed a towel over his head as he reached for the phone. "Hello?" All he heard was a dial tone.

After he hung up and put on his pants, he heard Eddie coming up the stairs. LeMar stepped out into the hallway.

"Hey, what's up?" Eddie's room was in the other direction.

"Nothing, man, just making sure somebody's not walking out with more of my belongings." He gave Eddie a long look. He didn't want to believe what the police had said, but since the break-in, Eddie hadn't been around much.

"Yeah, well, have you heard anything from the police yet?"

"Man, you know that stuff is as good as sold. I'll never get it back."

Eddie lowered his head. "That's a shame."

"It sure is." LeMar hesitated, waiting to see if Eddie wanted to tell him anything. If he knew anything, it might slip out. Instead, he just looked around, shaking his head.

"You getting dressed to go out?"

"Yeah, I've got a date."

"Cool, it's about time you started getting out. Is it one of those honeys you work with?"

LeMar stepped back into his room to continue dressing. Eddie stood in the doorway with his hands in his pockets.

"Believe it or not, she's a friend of Rosie's, and dig this, Rosie introduced us."

"You're kidding."

"Nope. I don't know what makes her think I need to be hooked up, but I'll play along with her little game. In fact, I'll give her more than she bargained for."

"What's this chick look like?"

"She's a nice-looking sista. Brown skin, shoulder-length wavy hair, and a very, very nice body."

"Oh, man. I don't believe this."

"What?"

"Sharon? Is her name Sharon?"

LeMar buttoned his shirt and sat down to tie his shoes. "Yeah, you know her?"

"Do I. Just don't mention my name to her. We're not the best of friends."

"Eddie, who *do* you get along with?"

"Anybody but women, it looks like."

Rosie finally got around to calling Kitty, the acquaintance of hers and Neville's.

"I should be getting a call any day now. You know, Susan has a good friend who works for the magazine, and she let it slip that I'd been selected."

Rosie wanted to stick her finger in the back of her throat. Kitty was so full of herself it turned Rosie's stomach. She found herself wishing she hadn't made the call.

"Well, I guess I'll have to wait and see."

"Rosie, I don't think you have anything to worry about. I saw that law office over on Peachtree that you decorated. It was different, you know, very ethnic."

Was that an insult? "Thank you, Kitty, I'm glad you liked it. It's called ethnocentric."

"Oh, I did, I did. That's how I know you're a shoo-in to be selected. *Design House* magazine is going to narrow it down to five Atlanta designers."

"Oh, I thought it was ten."

"No, they've changed it this year. They'll photograph our latest projects and do a spread in the magazine. I can't wait, I'm working on this little . . ."

Rosie didn't hear another word Kitty said. What current project of hers would look good photographed if she were one of the finalists? She didn't have one. The Colony House was too plain. LeMar's house would be perfect, only it wasn't close to being completed.

"How about you? What stunning project are you working on?" Kitty asked.

"An older home in Ansley Park."

"How wonderful. Whose is it, some rich corporate type?"

"You could say that. I'm doing a very rich-looking ethnocentric decor, and you know that's my specialty. It'll look great in a photo layout." It was about time Rosie became full of herself. She was just as good a designer as Kitty, if not better.

"Yes, that would look nice," Kitty said apprehensively. "We'll probably be competing for a spot in the magazine."

"We just might be." Rosie laughed to herself. Didn't Kitty just tell her that she was a shoo-in? Now she wasn't so sure.

"Kitty, I've really gotta run, but good luck."

She hung up more eager than ever to finish LeMar's house and hopefully use it in the layout. She had no idea if she'd be selected as a finalist. She had to get Neville back over to LeMar's house and shift things into high gear. He hadn't returned to work, nor had she heard from him. She picked up the phone to call him.

* * *

"Rosie, I'm sorry. I didn't mean to bail on you like that. I just didn't know how to tell you. And I didn't know if you'd heard it from someone else."

"Neville, tell me what?" She hoped he wasn't sick.

"I had an altercation with his houseguest."

"You what?" She couldn't believe her ears.

"LeMar's friend, Eddie. He came into the kitchen and started in on me. Then, for no reason at all, he hit me."

Stunned, she jumped from her seat. "You've got to be kidding!"

"I wish I was. We had words, then I left."

"Neville. No!" she said with a startled gasp. "I am so sorry." She held her hand over her mouth.

"It's not your fault. That little asshole did it, not you."

Leaning over with her elbow on the table, Rosie rested her forehead in the palm of her hand. Nothing like this had happened since she'd been in business.

"Why didn't you tell me? Is that why you called in sick?"

"I know how much the business means to you, so I figured I'd give the guy time to move out."

"Trust me, I'll take care of it. I'll have a talk with LeMar. We won't go back into that house until Eddie leaves. LeMar will have to put him out."

"I didn't mean to cause you any trouble or mess up the first time you let me fly solo."

"Neville, you didn't mess up. Nobody treats one of my employees that way. It'll all be taken care of, and you can still finish the house. Trust me."

* * *

Sharon met Rosie for their usual lunch date. This time she had good news for her. "Here's your check from my boss, Mr. Michalski."

"Thank you so much, Sharon. Girl, you came through for me." Rosie accepted the envelope and peeked inside at the amount. Sharon had a generous boss.

"Did you have any doubts? I told you he likes giving money to charity."

Rosie didn't really want to talk about the donation; she wanted to know about the date. The suspense was killing her. Sharon hadn't given her any lengthy details like she normally gave about her dates.

"I've got a new sponsor that you might be interested in."

"Who?" Sharon asked before taking a bite of her salad.

"Phillip Hamilton," Rosie replied, and continued eating.

Sharon swallowed hard and looked up. "So, you guys went out and you talked him into sponsorship?"

"Actually, he was interested in being a sponsor. We didn't go out on a date per se. It was more of a networking function. We attended a reception of a good friend of his, and he introduced me to several more people who may become sponsors."

"That still sounds like a date to me."

"He wasn't interested in me that way, nor was I in him. We attended that reception together, that's all. Nothing like what you and LeMar did."

"Well, I hate to tell you, but we didn't have a rump-roaring time, either."

"What do you mean?"

"He's good-looking, but I couldn't wait for the date to end."

"Where did you guys go?" She wanted all the details.

"Dave and Buster's. He wanted me to ride one of those motorcycle games in a dress. Can you believe it? I was prepared for a romantic evening at the Imperial Fuzz or a jazz club maybe, not acting like a sixteen-year-old."

"Sharon, you don't like Dave and Buster's? It's a lot of fun. You could have shot some pool, too."

"I'm not into shooting pool, or playing games. I wanted some jazz and maybe a decent dinner. Not chicken fingers and fries."

"I'm sorry, I really hoped you two would hit it off." Rosie fought to keep the smile from her face. If she were chewing, Sharon wouldn't be able to tell she wanted to smile, so she heaved a fork full of salad into her mouth.

"Now I see why you weren't so gung ho about him. He must have bored you to death. Girl, all he talked about was his job. And I was not interested in computer talk all night."

"You didn't go anywhere afterward?"

"After all that excitement, I had a headache. I went home and called a girlfriend of mine, and we went out."

"I wondered how it went, but you weren't saying anything."

"Well, I know he's an old friend of yours, and I didn't want to disappoint you, but I don't think we'll be going on a second date. Thanks anyway for trying to fix me up."

"You're welcome. You know I'm always looking out for you, girl."

Sharon pushed her salad aside and cleared her palate with some soda. "You know, you could try again."

Rosie looked at her in surprise. Did Sharon want

her to try with LeMar again? "You just said you didn't think there'd be a second date."

"I'm not talking about him. I'm talking about Phillip Hamilton. You know him now, and you said you two didn't go on a date. So, hook me up, girlfriend."

For a brief moment Rosie was jealous. Did Sharon want every man she met? Phillip was good-looking and just the thing to keep her mind off LeMar. Unfortunately, she knew he was in love with someone: himself.

"I'll tell you what. The next time I talk to him, I'll see if he's seeing anyone. If not, I'll mention you."

"No, why can't you set it up like you did with LeMar. We talked about you, you know. That was real smooth."

Rosie laughed. "I don't know if I can do that with Phillip. We're not old friends or anything." She thought about it for a few minutes as she finished her salad. "Let me make sure he's available, and I'll see what I can do."

"Thank you." Sharon was in better spirits. "Now that's the kind of man I need."

They spent the rest of their lunch talking about everything from the dance to their work problems.

Before Neville returned to work on LeMar's house, Rosie wanted to talk to LeMar about Eddie. The contractors had completed most of their work in the basement, so she took LeMar on a walk-through of everything completed so far. They discussed the progress and any changes he wanted to make.

Once the contractor left, she felt free to talk about Eddie. They sat in the kitchen finishing up a cup of coffee.

"LeMar, there's one more thing I wanted to talk to you about."

He held out his hand. "If it's about your friend Sharon, I'm sorry that didn't work out."

"No, it's not about her. It's about Eddie."

LeMar let out a sigh. "What did he do?"

"You know he did something, don't you?"

He shrugged. "It's his nature, I guess."

"Well, he's gone too far. He got into an argument with Neville the last time he was here, then he hit him."

He jumped back in his seat and shook his head, indicating she was wrong. "No way."

"I'm afraid he did."

"Why would he do that? Neville's bigger than Eddie."

"I don't know, but I can't finish this house with him here. I won't have Neville work with him around."

"I know Eddie's a little rough around the edges, but—"

"He's more than rough. LeMar, he's dangerous. Neville should have kicked his butt. Eddie makes me uncomfortable. I don't like the way he looks at me, insinuates little things, and tries to hit on me while I'm here working."

The air in the room changed. She'd said something that struck a nerve with him.

"He hits on you while you're here?"

She nodded. "And you call him your friend. Would a friend do that?"

He laughed it off. "Rosie, he's only doing it because he knows you don't like him. Don't let him get to you."

"Too late, he's gotten to me. Neville, too. I need

to know if you're going to do anything about it. If not, it may be impossible for us to finish the house."

"Look, I don't want anything to jeopardize you completing the house on schedule. Let me talk to Eddie and at least get his side of the story. I might have to remind him that his time is up."

"I know he's your buddy and all, and you take care of him like a little brother, but, LeMar, he's bad news. Can't you see he's never going to change?"

"He's just had some bad luck. He's not a bad guy. When his mom passed away he got involved with the wrong crowd, but he'll straighten up his act."

"I hope so, and I hope he doesn't bring you down with him before he does."

He smiled and shook his head. "He can't do that. If my life takes a turn for the worse, I won't be able to blame anyone but myself. I'm my own man. I'm not a follower."

"Well, I can't have him being abusive toward my employee. I'm surprised Neville didn't call the police. I would have."

"Then I thank you for coming to me and giving me a chance to straighten him out."

"LeMar, I told Neville we wouldn't start working again until Eddie was gone. I know I can't tell you what to do about him, but I need for you to do more than talk to him."

He held up his hand. "Don't worry. It won't happen again, and I'll apologize to Neville myself."

She sipped her coffee, but it was cold. She pushed the mug aside, then picked up her briefcase to leave.

"Thank you. I'd hate for Eddie to jeopardize the completion of this job. As it is, he's already caused a delay."

"What is it with him? Even your friend Sharon doesn't like him."

"You guys talked about Eddie?"

"No, Eddie admitted to not being one of her favorite people. I guess I'm not either right now."

"I'm sorry you guys didn't hit it off. I thought you would have looked good together."

He raised his left brow and stared at her. "Really?"

"I think so."

"I disagree with you. She's not at all my type. I prefer somebody who's not so high-maintenance and knows how to have a good time."

Rosie gave a little laugh. "Sharon can be high-maintenance." She started walking slowly out of the kitchen.

He followed her. "You know how we used to compete at the campus game room all the time, then I'd beat you bad at a couple of games of pool?"

"Wait a minute. You never beat me that bad. And if I recall correctly, I beat you most of the time. We only kept competing so you could try to surpass me in wins."

He shrugged as he followed her to the front door. "What can I say, I'm a competitive type of guy. I hate to lose. You should remember that."

"Oh, yes, how could I forget. If I beat you two games to three, we had to play at least two more games before I went back to my dorm. It was pathetic."

"Hey, my competitiveness and love for a challenge has gotten me to the regional manager level at Skynet. So let's not knock it."

"Considering you're paying me right now, I won't. But it also got you in trouble a couple of times, if I remember correctly."

"Most important, it got me you. My biggest challenge in school was to get that pretty girl in my music class to notice me. After we met, you made me chase you."

Rosie stood with her hand on the doorknob and looked back at him. She sucked in her cheeks to keep from blushing. "Yeah, but you lost that competitive drive when you moved back to D.C. I guess you found another challenge."

He recoiled as if he'd been hit in the chest. "That's not exactly what happened."

"I'm sorry, I didn't mean to go there. That wasn't fair." How had she tripped back to memory lane? "Just forget what I said, and I'm sorry again about Sharon. The next time—"

"Hold it. No. Let's not try that again." He met her at the door and grabbed the other side of the doorknob. "I appreciate it, but I'd prefer to find my own date. There's something about having your . . . friend hook you up with her friends. You know what I mean?"

"Yeah, I guess." Time stood still as they held the doorknob looking at each other. She wanted to know what he was thinking. Memories of him sneaking up to her dorm room in the middle of the night flashed through her mind. She cursed at herself to stop.

"So, I'm not available, until you're available."

She let go of the doorknob as if it were on fire. Then she held up her hand, displaying a gold band. "I'm not available, remember?"

He snapped his fingers. "Right, I keep forgetting. I prefer to remember us together."

Twelve

LeMar pulled into the driveway, returning from the car wash. He popped the trunk and pulled out a rag to wipe down the car again. Music from the car radio echoed out of the trunk. He sang along with the music as a small sports car pulled up and Eddie jumped out.

"Hey, where you been?" LeMar hadn't seen him in a couple of days.

Eddie walked over, looking as if he hadn't slept. "Man, I meant to call you. I had to run to Columbus."

LeMar stopped. He knew Eddie's father lived in Columbus. "Everything okay?"

"My old man's sick. I went by Kim's house the other day, and she gave me the message."

"How's he doing?"

"He's got cancer. So he wanted to see everybody like we were some close-knit family. I hadn't seen him in more than seven years, but he wanted to talk to me."

"I'm sorry to hear that. I hope it's not terminal."

Eddie shrugged and cleared his throat. "I think it is. He's lost a lot of weight, and he's looking pretty bad. But I guess every dog has his day. Maybe this is payback for the way he treated my mom before she died. Beating our asses wasn't good enough, he had to beat her, too. Once he kicked me out, he didn't have to ever worry about seeing me again."

He'd heard Eddie's dysfunctional family stories before. His father had been abusive, and his mother had been submissive.

"Hey, man, I need to ask you about something."

"Yeah."

"Rosie was by yesterday. She told me about you and Neville."

"Aw, man. Look, I'm sorry. I didn't mean to go off on him like that, but I can't stand no punk man."

"I don't want to hear that. You didn't have to hit him."

"What?" He gave LeMar a stunned look. "I didn't hit him. Man, I pushed him out of my way. That's all."

The incriminating look in Eddie's eyes rubbed LeMar the wrong way. Why was he lying to him? Apparently, he'd changed a lot more than LeMar had realized.

"Say, man, just don't let it happen again. Maybe you should be out looking for work in the morning anyway, then you guys won't bump heads."

"I've got a line on something."

"Good. You and your girl hooking back up?" It was time for him to leave. LeMar wanted him to make the move instead of making him feel kicked out.

"We're talking. When I stopped by she asked me where I'd been staying. But if you're ready for me to leave, I can get out of your way this weekend. Man, I know I've stayed longer than I intended to."

"I want you to get yourself together. Man, what's going on with you? I don't see you that much, then when I do you look like you've been sleeping in a car."

Eddie shook his head. "Out here trying to make a little money."

"Legally, I hope?"

"Of course. Have you ever known me to get myself in too much trouble? Don't answer that." He held out his hand while they both laughed.

"Okay, let's just say I'm not going to do anything dumb. I've got a plan I'm working on, and in a couple of days I should be set and able to get out of your way."

LeMar shook his head. "If you need my help with anything, just let me know."

"Thanks, man." They shook hands. "I know you've always got my back. I appreciate it. And that goes both ways. If you ever need me, let me know."

"So, I can tell Rosie that everything's straightened out? No more problems with Neville?"

"Yeah, I'm cool."

"Great. Just make yourself scarce during the morning hours until you move, that's all I ask."

"Okay, I don't want to mess up anything between you and your little lady friend. I know how you're still sweating her and everything."

LeMar returned to rubbing down his car. "She's a married woman."

"Yeah, but what's that got to do with anything?"

LeMar turned to Eddie, who winked and smiled at him.

A week later, Rosie and LeMar stood on his front lawn, admiring the landscapers' work.

"This looks real good. I like how they made it low-maintenance, too. No flowers to plant, and all that stuff. I love it."

"Thank you. I'm glad you're satisfied."

"I'm more than satisfied, I'm thrilled."

"Well, we're a little behind schedule, but we're making progress. That's one completed part of the project."

"You know, this calls for a celebration. Let's go inside."

"I'm sorry, I really don't have time, I've got to get over to—"

"Aw come on, it'll only take a second." He took the steps two at a time with her reluctantly following.

In the kitchen he pulled out a bottle of wine. He saw the apprehension on her face, but he was determined to have a drink with her.

"Grab two glasses from over there for me." He pointed to the cabinet that held his wineglasses, then he uncorked the wine.

She moved slowly. "Oh, LeMar, I don't have time for a drink. I really need to run."

He pretended not to hear her over the loud popping of the cork. "Get the glasses with the twisted-looking stem, those are my favorites."

She stared at him, then slowly walked over to grab the glasses. "Okay, one drink. That's all I have time for."

He poured her less than half a glass of wine and held up his glass. "Let's have a toast."

She hesitated, but then held up her glass.

"To the best designer, decorator, and whatever other talents you have, in town." He touched his glass to hers. "Cheers."

"Cheers." She sipped the wine and eyed LeMar over the rim of her glass.

He looked down into his glass. "Do you remember the last time we made a toast?"

"Yeah, that was years ago."

"We celebrated our two-year anniversary at the Omega Purple-and-Gold Ball," he said, looking up at her.

"I remember the three-dollar bottle of wine we celebrated with, because it gave me a headache the next morning."

"Hey, I was a college man. I couldn't afford the expensive stuff then."

Silence fell over the room. LeMar finished his glass and poured himself another. He held the bottle to refill Rosie's glass.

She held out her hand in protest. "No, thank you. One's enough for me. I've got another job to work on after I leave here."

He held up the bottle. "You're not going to make me finish this bottle all by myself, are you?" He turned his lips down and gave her a sad face. "Come on, one more glass."

"This was supposed to be about business. Now you're trying to get me drunk."

Before she could protest again, he poured a little more. She hadn't finished her first glass. "Never. Besides, I haven't even poured you a full glass. Let's go in the den. I want to show you something."

"Okay, I'll let you talk me into one more glass." She followed him into the den. "After all, you did get rid of Eddie for me. If I haven't already, I want to thank you for that."

"He didn't actually move out. I made it clear that he had to stay out of your way." He picked up the remote and turned on the stereo before setting his glass on a side table. "But he should be moved out by next week."

"Have a seat." He motioned to the couch.

"I know Neville hasn't seen him, so we thought he moved out. Thanks for having a talk with him, then."

LeMar pulled a book from the built-in bookcase and walked over to her. "I was unpacking some boxes the other day and found this." He flipped through a photo album to a picture of them at a football game together.

LeMar caught the smile on her face and knew the picture would bring back pleasant memories. It happened to be one of the happiest times of his life. She had on his baseball cap, and they had wrapped themselves up in a blanket.

"So, how many old pictures of us do you have?" After looking at the picture, she set the album on the couch beside her.

He sat down next to the photo album. "A few. That one brings back some good memories." He shrugged and sipped his wine. "It actually fell out of the book when I picked it up earlier today."

She laughed. "You had me worried for a minute there. I thought maybe you were going to break out a whole book of old pictures of us."

"No. There's a few more in there, but we didn't take a lot of pictures. I just wanted to toast the first completed phase of the renovation. Then I remembered the photo." He walked over to put the album back on the shelf.

Rosie took another sip of her wine. She'd actually wanted to flip through the photo album to see if he had a picture of his girlfriend in Maryland.

He returned to the sofa and sat down. "So, what job are you running to after you leave here?"

She didn't really have to run. "I'm decorating a house that Colony Homes is donating to a homeless family. I need to run by and see if one of my sponsors came through with some things he promised me."

"I remember you telling be about that. How's it coming?"

"Good. I could use another sponsor to really make it look good, but it's a labor of love."

"This sounds like a pro bono-type deal. You're not going to make any money off it?"

"Not directly. I did it for the first time last year. A few weeks after the event I usually get some referrals. But that's not why I do it."

"I know it's not. You've got a good heart. That's one of the things that I loved about you."

She finished as much wine as she was going to drink. She set the glass on the coffee table. "Well, my good heart struggles to get enough sponsors, but each year it will probably get easier."

"You know, I might be able to help you out. I had lunch with some guys the other day who were talking about ways to get more exposure for their company. Your project might be right for them. They get exposure, and it's for a good cause."

"That sounds good. Thank you." The sips of wine seemed to have loosened her mind a bit. She found herself being distracted by the way LeMar sat back on the couch with his arm stretched over the back. She wanted to lean over and rest her head against his chest. His cologne was intoxicating and working her along with the music in the background. This was getting a little too comfortable. Time to leave before she did something she'd regret.

"I'll give you a call this week to put you in touch with somebody," he offered.

She stood to leave. "Great, and this time I really do have to go. Thanks for the drink."

He stood to walk her out. "You're welcome. We'll

have to do it again once the whole house is completed."

"Sure."

She turned to shake his hand and say good night, but before she could say anything, he leaned over and kissed her on the cheek.

"Thanks again, I'll see you later."

Speechless, she nodded and walked down the steps. Maybe two glasses of wine were too much for him, too.

Doreece had waited for more than an hour for Rosie. She tried calling her cellular phone but didn't get an answer. They were supposed to put up the border and install some shelves in the Colony House.

When Tony finally called to say he wanted to see her, Doreece needed to leave. She wrote Rosie a note and left it in the middle of the living-room floor. She knew her sister would understand her wanting to settle some issues with missing in action Tony. He picked her up, and she left her car at the Colony House.

"Thanks for agreeing to have dinner with me."

Doreece kept her distance, leaning more toward the passenger's-side door. "You said you wanted to talk."

"Yeah." He let out a long sigh. "I don't want you to think I'm trying to run away from my responsibility or anything. It's real hard for me to deal with this when I know that you were seeing somebody else."

"Tony, I told you—"

"I know, you weren't intimate with him. I believe you, it's just taken me some time to admit that. In the back of my mind I had doubts, and that's what

I want to talk to you about. If you don't mind, I've fixed dinner at my place so we can talk."

Finally, he was coming around. She knew he wasn't a no-good dog as Rosie wanted her to believe. He just needed some time. She was in better spirits herself.

"Your place is fine with me."

Thirteen

Late Saturday night, LeMar was cleaning up the kitchen when something shiny caught his attention. Above the sink in a small glass dish in which he kept his keys was a ring.

He picked up the gold band and knew right away that it was Rosie's wedding ring. The last couple of evenings he'd worked late and hadn't caught her or Neville at the house.

He pocketed the ring and made a mental note to return it before he left town the next day. How long had the ring been there? And why hadn't she missed it?

Sunday afternoon, with his bags packed and ready for his five o'clock flight to New York, LeMar found Rosie's address and went to return her ring. With any luck, he'd also get to meet her husband.

He pulled up to the tidy house with its immaculately manicured yard and got out. It looked like her, he thought. He got out and walked up to the front door. After ringing the bell a few times and getting no response, he realized he should have called first. Now what was he going to do? He didn't want to take the ring all the way to New York with him.

"Honey, can I help you with something? She's out at the moment."

He turned around to see an elderly woman sitting in a chair on the porch next door. Had she been there when he'd pulled up? He didn't think so.

"I was trying to catch Rosie. Guess I should have called first."

"Yes, she's over at her mother's right now."

"Hmm." He stood there contemplating whether he should return home and leave the ring there. If he did, he might miss his flight.

"Is there something I can do for you?"

"Actually, there is." He crossed the driveway to Rosie's neighbor's house. She met him at the top of the steps.

"My name's LeMar Reed. She's decorating my house for me."

"Oh, yes, she's told me about the house. It's in Ansley Park, right?"

"Yes, ma'am." He blinked in surprise.

"Rosie and I are very close. She's like a daughter to me, you see, so I know about most of her clients."

He shook his head. That explained why Rosie had been talking about his house.

"If it wouldn't be too much trouble"—he reached into his pants pocket and pulled out the ring— "could you give this to her? I found it in the kitchen where I guess she was working. I'm on my way to catch a flight to New York, and I'd hate to take it with me."

Carrie took the ring and held it in the palm of her hand. "Well, if it isn't her wedding ring."

"She's probably going crazy wondering where she lost it. I'm on my way out of town, but I wanted to return it before Rosie or her husband got upset about it missing."

Carrie laughed and put the ring into her dress pocket. "Honey, he doesn't even live in Atlanta. He'd never know if she lost it."

He swallowed what felt like a rock caught in his throat. He coughed to clear it. "Excuse me? He doesn't live with her?"

"Why, no, they've been divorced for more than two years now. David's my nephew. They made a very nice couple, but they weren't too compatible."

He hoped she didn't recognize the astounded look on his face. LeMar remembered now. He couldn't believe Rosie had led him to believe she was still married.

"I'm sorry, I didn't catch your name," he said, trying not to look so stunned.

"Carrie Evans." She held out her hand to shake his. "Honey, is something wrong?"

"No ma'am, uh . . . I didn't know about the divorce. I'm sorry to hear about it. I hope it wasn't too upsetting for her?" Since this woman had a gift for gab, he might as well see what she wanted to share.

She crossed her arms. "You went to school with her, didn't you?"

"Yes, ma'am. We attended Clark Atlanta together."

"Did you know my nephew, David Wright?"

LeMar thought about it, but couldn't remember him. "No, ma'am, I don't believe I did. The name doesn't ring a bell."

"He attended Clark also. That's Rosie's ex-husband. He's a nice young man. They had a peaceful divorce, and they've remained friends. I'm sure Rosie is doing fine."

"That's good to hear. Well, I guess I better run. Thank you, and if you would, please let her know I returned the ring."

"I sure will, and it was a pleasure meeting you."

He stepped down one step, then stopped. "Mrs. Evans, could you not share with Rosie that you told me she was divorced. If we can keep that between us, I'd appreciate it. I'm sure she's going to tell me in her own time."

She gave him a sideways glance. "Honey, just how close were you two in college?"

"You can say we were extremely close for more than two years."

"Uh-huh, well, I don't see why she didn't tell you she was divorced, if you were that close."

"Neither do I."

"Are you single?"

He chuckled. "Yes, ma'am, I am." She reminded him of his mother. Direct, up-front, and sassy for her age.

"Good, good. I won't mention anything to Rosie as long as you don't mention to her that I let the cat out of the bag. You know, she's not dating anyone at the moment. You should ask her out."

He shrugged. "I'd love to, but she wants me to believe she's married for some reason. I can only assume that she doesn't want to go out with me."

"Oh, honey, some women don't know what's good for them unless it hits them over the head. Come on up here and have a seat, we need to talk."

He glanced at his watch. "I guess I can spare a few minutes before I need to leave for the airport." He took a seat on the porch next to her, not knowing what to expect.

LeMar raised his tray table into the upright position and fastened his seat belt. This was going to be a long flight. He had too much on his mind. He needed to concentrate on his Monday morning meeting. However, all he could think about was Rosie.

Why had she deliberately lied to him? She'd gone as far as to hold up her hand and say, "I got married and went on with my life." He couldn't understand it; she had no reason to lie to him.

He closed his eyes as the plane started down the runway. Since flying wasn't one of his favorite things, he said his usual prayer before takeoff.

Carrie had gotten out of him that in college he and Rosie had been a couple. She seemed to take a liking to him, and he had a feeling he'd be thankful for that someday. She definitely cared about Rosie. Her concern was that Rosie worked too much and never seemed to have fun. At least, he gathered as much from her rambling conversation.

He had to find a way to get Rosie to admit she was divorced. He wanted to hear it from her lips. He wanted her to face him and tell him why she lied to him, of all people.

After the flight attendant gave him his peanuts and glass of soda, he stretched his feet out as best he could. Leaving his seat belt on, he reclined his seat a bit and rested his eyes again.

As he drifted off to sleep, thoughts of his past and Rosie surfaced. She'd been upset when he'd gone back to D.C., but he hadn't thought their relationship would end. He'd spent weeks taking care of family business and trying to catch Rosie on the phone between classes. As time had passed, the distance between them had grown. Then she'd cut him off. Without any explanation at all, she'd refused his calls.

After a couple of months, he'd tracked her down. . . .

"Ray, thanks a lot, man, I've been trying to get Rosie's number for weeks."

"No problem. I haven't seen her in a long time, but I got it from a girlfriend of hers. Man, I knew you two would be getting married if anybody would. Especially after the way you guys walked around campus like you were joined at the hip."

"I don't know about all that. Right now, I think she's upset because I needed to transfer to Howard, and I won't be back to Atlanta this semester."

"Okay, let me know when you get down this way again."

"Will do. Later." He hung up and stared at Rosie's number for a while. He'd gone through everything to get it. She'd instructed her mother and little sister not to give him her number. His attempts at persuading them had failed. Finally, he'd called on one of his fraternity brothers to help him out.

He was back in his old bedroom staring at a picture of Rosie and him on his dresser. He didn't care if she was dating somebody else; he picked up the phone and dialed her number.

After every ring, he wanted to hang up. What if she hung up on him? Even worse, what if she told him she didn't want to ever see him again? He didn't think he could take that. He already wanted to be with her again.

After the fourth ring, he heard a grumbling sound on the other end.

"Hello."

LeMar sat up in bed, his eyes wide. A man's voice came from the other end. Maybe he had the wrong number?

"Hello," he said again, this time louder.

"May I speak to Rosie?" There was always a chance the guy was a relative.

The man on the phone cleared his throat and seemed to move the phone from his ear. Then he came back. *"She's asleep. Who's calling?"*

So he had the right number. *"A friend of hers. Who is this?"*

"David, her husband."

Husband! The word rang in LeMar's ear. He stood up. No way. He had the wrong Rosie.

"I'm calling for Rosie Greene. Is this the right number?" He had to have the wrong number. He felt a tightness in his chest, and it became more and more difficult to breathe.

"Yeah, it's Rosie Wright now. Who is this?" he asked, sounding annoyed.

LeMar stopped breathing and slammed the phone down. What the hell is going on! How could she be married? He'd only been in D.C. for three months. He sat down, his heartbeat so loud he feared his mother would hear it downstairs.

Completely at a loss, he turned up the stereo and laid back on the bed. A teardrop rolled from the corner of his eye. He couldn't believe it; his whole world was falling apart. . . .

The pilot came on and announced that they were approaching New York. LeMar raised his seat back and looked out the window. His heart still hurt from the dream. He remembered that night as if it were yesterday. He'd never called Rosie's house again.

Rosie picked Doreece up early Monday morning so they could get a little shopping in before she had to take Carrie to the grocery store. Neville was working on LeMar's house, so she had a little free time.

They wound up in the baby department. Rich's department store was having a one-day sale, and Doreece wanted Rosie to help her pick out baby clothes.

"Why don't you wait until after your baby shower before you start buying clothes?" Rosie asked, not really wanting to spend too much time in the baby department.

"I can't." She held up a little pink dress with ruffles. "Isn't this cute?"

Rosie nodded and ran her hand across the dress.

"Come on, help me pick out some outfits. These are cute, but let's look at infant clothes. I don't know if it's a girl or a boy."

"Are you going to find out?"

"I was, but Tony doesn't want to know. He said we should let it be a surprise."

"I'm glad he's come around."

"I told you he would. He knows this baby is his, and he's going to be a daddy. He's actually a little excited."

Rosie walked over to a rack of little-boy baseball outfits and wanted to cry. She'd had a little boy. She wanted to have another baby. She wanted to be married and start a family.

"Oh, look at this." Doreece pulled Rosie away from the clothes into a section that displayed room decorations.

Rosie followed her and tried to be as supportive as she could. "So what do you have in mind for the baby's room?"

"I like this." Doreece pointed to a Betty Boop bedspread.

"Betty Boop. Girl, you remind me of Jimmy wanting to paint those naked angels."

Doreece snapped her fingers. "You gave me a great idea. I'll get Jimmy to do me Betty Boop on the wall. Those angels he did turned out nicely, didn't they?"

"Once he toned them down, they worked fine. He's really good."

"You know, we need to have a drink at lunch to celebrate. The Colony House is almost complete."

"Doreece, you can't drink anything. We'll toast with a glass of iced tea. Did I tell you that Phillip Hamilton's agent called, and he wants Phillip to be at the open-house ceremony? Actually, he said he has to be there, and he needs to have his picture taken with the family for publicity purposes."

"He has to?"

"That's what he said. I owe it to him in exchange for his sponsorship. He has such a good heart, doesn't he?"

Doreece laughed. "Yeah, he's a real role model. I'm glad you two didn't hit it off."

"You and me both. But I think I've got the girl for him. Sharon and LeMar didn't hit it off, but Phillip is more her speed. I need to find a way to introduce them."

"Invite Sharon to the open-house ceremony. They can hook up at the afterparty. We're still celebrating at Justin's, aren't we?"

"That's a good idea. Yeah, I've invited everybody that helped with the project. It's going to be a fun night."

They left Rich's and visited a few more stores before Doreece purchased enough baby clothes to satisfy herself. Rosie felt better about looking at baby clothes before the day was over with.

She looked at her watch. "Doreece, I've got to pick Mrs. Carrie up in an hour. Thanks for dragging me through the baby department. I guess I needed it, whether I knew it or not."

"Sure, Auntie Rosie."

Rosie liked the sound of it, and the idea of being an aunt.

* * *

Carrie was ready and waiting when Rosie rang the bell.

"What's in the pouch?" Rosie asked.

"Coupons. I've been clipping them out of the paper. I've got to start cutting back. This month I spent too much money, and I don't know on what."

"If you need some help with something, let me know." Rosie held the door open for her.

"No, honey, I'm okay." She stopped in the doorway. "Oh, just a minute, I forgot something." She stepped back inside the house for a minute, then returned.

After locking the door, she turned to Rosie. "Have you missed something?"

"Huh?" Rosie looked down at her outstretched hand.

Carrie held Rosie's wedding band in her palm.

Rosie's mouth flew open, and she looked down at her hand. "My ring!"

"Had you missed it?"

She took the ring and put it on her finger. "No, I hadn't. I don't wear it all the time, so I forgot I'd put it back on. Where did you find it?"

"Mr. Reed came by yesterday to return it. He found it in his kitchen."

They walked out to the car. "My god, I can't believe that I took my ring off and left it anywhere."

"He couldn't believe it, either."

Driving to the grocery story, Rosie questioned Carrie about LeMar's visit. She wanted to know how he'd come to leave the ring with her.

"I told him I'd make sure you got it. He was on his way out of town. He seems like a nice young man."

"So you talked with him?"

"Yes, he sat on the porch, and we visited for a while."

Rosie looked over at her slowly. Oh, no, they'd talked, and Carrie loved to talk. What all could she have told him?

"How long was he there?"

"I don't know, not long. He had to catch a plane."

They rode on in silence for a few minutes. Rosie had a suspicion that more had transpired. Carrie was too quiet.

"He didn't ask you any personal questions about me, did he?"

"No, why do you ask?"

"I was just wondering."

"We hardly mentioned you at all."

She was in trouble. There was no way Carrie could sit alone with LeMar and not talk about her. In time she was sure she'd find out how much damage had been done.

Fourteen

"Rosie, your interpretation of contemporary African design is stunning. The way you've incorporated elements of African art throughout this house is truly astonishing." Doreece strolled through LeMar's living room in awe.

"Thank you. Everything's not from Africa; some of this is African-inspired. The mural behind the couch was painted by a local artist."

"How come I didn't see any of this stuff when it came in?"

They walked out into the hallway. "I had most of it shipped here and not to the office." Rosie pointed at the rug on the hardwood floor. "That carpet's inspired by the West African weaving traditions. It's by James Jufenkian."

"Girl, LeMar's in for a surprise when he gets back in town. When did he say he was coming back?"

"Actually, he didn't. I guess he'll be back one day this week. I didn't get a chance to talk to him before he left on Sunday. He came by the house but I wasn't there. You'll never guess what I did?"

Doreece walked through the hall, looking up and around at the artwork and masks. "What?"

"I walked off and left my wedding band in his

kitchen one day. That's why he came by, to return it, then he left it with Mrs. Carrie."

"Oh, Lordy, there's no telling what all she talked about. I know you guys are close and everything, but that's one gossiping old woman. Let her know your business, and she'll tell everybody she knows."

"She's just lonely."

"Yeah, well, don't tell her any of my business. I don't want it in the street."

"Come on, let me show you the rest of the house right quick." Doreece's words gave Rosie a sick feeling. Mrs. Carrie had probably told LeMar about her divorce.

They ended the tour in the kitchen.

"I've got some ceramic tiles with West African Adinka symbols and patterns that I'm going to put over here." She pointed to the wall behind the stove. "Also over by this window." As she looked out the back window, she heard the front door open. She cursed under her breath. She had hoped to be out of the house before Eddie showed up.

Doreece heard the door, too. She stood up. "I guess we better be getting out of here."

"It's probably Eddie. He's an old friend of LeMar's who's been staying here, but I thought he was moving out. Come on." They left the kitchen.

Standing in the foyer was LeMar with his suitcase before him and the mail in his hand. He stared at Rosie without saying a word. She had a key, but that look made her feel as if she shouldn't be there.

"Hi, LeMar. I was finishing up, didn't expect you." Doreece was right on her heels.

"Hi. Yeah, I got in a little while ago."

She held her hand out, sweeping it about. "Well, phase two is complete. Most of the African art's added. Look around and let me know what you think."

He dropped the mail on the hall table and picked up his suitcase. "I'm a little tired right now. I'll check it out later." He looked from Rosie to Doreece.

"This is my sister, Doreece." Rosie introduced them.

"Hello. I love your house. It's wonderful."

"Thank you. If you ladies will excuse me, I need to unpack. You can let yourself out, can't you?"

"Sure," Rosie said, slightly hurt. *What has gotten into him?* She watched him as he climbed the stairs and turned the corner.

She looked back at Doreece. "I guess we better go. Come on." They walked into the den and grabbed their purses.

Once they were outside, Doreece asked, "Man, what's wrong with him? Is he always like that?"

"No, never. He must have had a bad trip. After phase one he wanted to have a drink to celebrate. He usually wants to walk around and see what I did. Yeah, it was probably the trip. I wish we hadn't been here when he came in." As they drove off, Rosie wondered about the strange look LeMar had given her.

Two days later, Rosie helped Neville complete the tiles in LeMar's kitchen. Out back she painted a pair of small tables she'd found at a flea market. Standing to take a break, she was startled by LeMar sitting on the back step.

"Hello, I didn't hear you come out. How long have you been sitting there?"

He stood and walked down the steps. "I just came out." He stepped over to examine the tables. "Nice paint job."

She held her brush, looking down at the tables. "I'm not finished yet, but thanks. They're for the kitchen."

"I appreciate you spending your Saturday morning here."

"We're a little behind, so I'm playing catch-up."

He circled her, and the tables, with his hands in his pockets.

"Did you go jogging this morning?" she asked.

He looked down at his warm-up suit. "No, I play basketball on Saturday mornings at the YMCA."

"That's good." He was still giving her a piercing look.

She continued painting while he stood over her. "Your husband doesn't mind you working here on a Saturday?"

She didn't look up. "I work plenty of Saturdays."

"He must be used to your hours then?"

She stopped and looked up again. "It's not exactly a nine-to-five job. Besides, I own the company, so I can pretty much work when I want." His nice little attitude was all gone. What had happened to him on that business trip? He hadn't smiled at her once since he'd been back.

"I'd like to meet your husband," he blurted out.

Her hand froze in midstroke. She heard him loud and clear. She continued to paint. "Sure."

"How about this weekend?"

Why is he pressuring me so much? "LeMar, you keep asking me questions about my husband—did you ever think maybe he doesn't want to meet you?" She was reaching, but he was so persistent.

"Where did you guys meet?"

"In school. Haven't we had this discussion before?" She dipped her paintbrush in a jar of cleaner.

"No, I don't think we have. You don't talk much about your marriage. Did I know him?"

So that's it. "No, you didn't."

"I've always been rather curious about who you married. I just want to make sure you're happy."

"I'm very happy, thank you. You don't have to be so concerned about me." Putting her paintbrush aside, she stood and brushed herself off. When she looked at LeMar, he glared back at her. He knew something, she was sure of it. She prayed Carrie hadn't talked too much.

"I'll let these tables dry out here. Tomorrow they'll be ready for a glaze, then into the kitchen. They make nice little accent tables."

He merely nodded, not taking his eyes off her.

Rosie went back into the house and left LeMar outside. He was making her uncomfortable again. If he knew about her divorce, why didn't he come right out and say something? She hated walking around not knowing if he knew. There was only one way for her to find out. She had to talk to Carrie.

When Rosie returned to her office, she picked up the phone and called her neighbor.

"Hello, Evans residence."

"Hi, Carrie, it's Rosie."

"Hi, honey. Is everything all right?"

"Oh, yeah, just fine. I need to ask you something."

"Sure."

"When LeMar came by to return my ring, did he ask you any questions about my marriage?"

"No, we talked about Atlanta and D.C."

"Are you sure?"

"Yes. I was very impressed with him, he's such a nice young man."

"What did he say about my ring particularly?" Maybe she told him without really knowing she'd told him. Rosie wanted to know everything they'd discussed.

"Honey, I already told you. He figured you were going crazy trying to find it. Then he gave it to me. Why? Is something wrong?"

"No, ma'am. I was curious, that's all."

"You know, I think he'd make a nice catch for you. I don't know why you didn't want to be around him."

"It's a long story. I'll let you go and get back to whatever you were doing." She hung up feeling partially confident that Carrie wouldn't have mentioned it if LeMar hadn't asked about her husband.

LeMar came home from work Thursday evening and saw that Eddie had his suitcase sitting at the bottom of the stairs. He originally wasn't going to move out until the weekend. LeMar hadn't wanted to push him out, but he couldn't expect to stay there forever.

LeMar walked back into the kitchen, where he found Eddie. "Hey, looks like you're getting ready to go." Eddie sat at the table eating his last free meal.

He had a mouth full. "Yeah—oh, man, I didn't hear you come in. I thought I'd go ahead and start tonight. I'll be back tomorrow to get the rest of my things. I didn't realize I had so much over here."

Yeah, you'd practically moved in. "Stuff accumulates fast. Man, I didn't mean to rush you—"

"Don't worry about it. It's time for me and Kim to get things straightened out anyway."

"Moving back in?"

"With her? No. I was going to share an apartment out in Lithonia with Dru, but he moved in with some chick. I got a place in Riverdale, down by the airport."

For a split second, and only a split second, LeMar felt like the bad guy. Throwing his buddy out in the street when he didn't really have a place to go.

"Man, it's probably best. I'm not too sure about that Dru character anyway. He looks like the type of guy you need to avoid."

"He's cool."

"What happened to your card games? I hope you gave them up."

"Oh, yeah, that's history. I got a job."

LeMar smiled and nodded. "Good, where at?"

"The airport." He finished off his sandwich and picked at his teeth with a knife.

"That's good. How'd you get the job?"

"This buddy of mine works out there. He hooked me up. It's not much, but it's a start. The card games were wearing me out. I'm not cut out for that sort of thing anyway."

LeMar was glad to hear him talking like he had some sense. It was time he grew up.

"Say, I need another favor. I hate to ask you this, man, but until I get my first check, I'm flat busted. Can you spot me about fifty dollars until payday? I'll pay you back as soon as I cash the check."

Never before had LeMar felt comfortable loaning Eddie money. But it seemed like he was trying to turn his life around. "Sure, I guess I can spot you. I'll be right back."

He told himself he might never get the money back, but he'd feel better about Eddie leaving if he had a little money to get him by. Hopefully, he'd never have to ask for money again.

* * *

"I want out, I told you." Eddie paced around the den on the phone. "I played my last game, I'm out. Man, I can't get caught up in no stuff like that." He looked out into the hall to make sure LeMar hadn't returned.

"Do what you want, just leave me out of it."

When LeMar came back downstairs, Eddie was in the den on the phone. He left the money on the table and carried his briefcase into his new downstairs office. Rosie hadn't finished the space yet, but it was complete enough for him to work. He'd also replaced his computer.

Eddie walked in after him. "Say, man, can you run me over to North Avenue? A buddy of mine took my car and worked on it. Now it's complete, but he can't get it to me. It'll only take a second."

LeMar looked down at his briefcase and thought about the work inside. But without a car, Eddie might not be able to leave.

"Sure, let me change clothes first." He went upstairs and changed into a sweat suit.

They left all of Eddie's things at the house and went to pick up his car. During the ride, Eddie brought up Rosie.

"She's got the house looking real good, man. That girl's got skills."

"Yeah, I'm impressed. She's actually done a better job than I expected. The place is starting to take shape."

"You know I saw her out the other night."

"Yeah, with who?" He couldn't resist asking.

"Her buddy, Sharon, and some other honey. It's too bad you guys couldn't get back together."

LeMar looked out his side window. "Yeah, too bad." He didn't even want to think about her right now.

"Did you ever talk to her about what happened after you left school?"

He let out a loud sigh. "Man, I don't want to talk about Rosie right now. I found out she's been lying to me about something."

"No kidding, what she lie about?"

LeMar looked over at him, wondering if he'd already known. "She's been divorced for more than two years."

"Get outta here!" Eddie leaned toward the car door. "What did she lie for?"

"I haven't found out yet, but I plan to."

Rosie walked through the Colony House, making sure everything was in place. In a few more days the new home-owners would be arriving. When she walked into the children's room, angels greeted her. It was perfect. Soft, subtle figures floating across the wall.

The house was almost complete, and the open-house ceremony was all planned. Colony Homes was footing the tab for the party afterward.

"Lunch is here." Doreece stuck her head into the room.

Rosie left the bedroom and went into the kitchen. "Great, I'm starved."

They ate and discussed the party plans. "I have to carry Mrs. Carrie out this afternoon to find a dress," Rosie shared.

"You're bringing her?"

"Of course, you know she doesn't get out enough."

"I'm bringing Tony."

"So, you two have patched things up?"

"We've pretty much worked things out."

"Doreece, I'm glad to hear that. Why didn't you tell me before?"

"Well, you know he's excited about the baby. But I didn't mention anything else to you because I know how you feel about him. I know how you feel about men in general."

"What are you trying to say?" Rosie stopped eating.

"You're afraid of men. Or you're afraid of commitment. One or the other."

"I am not." Rosie's voice rose as she looked at her sister in shock.

"Yes, you are. You don't date. Your ex-husband was more of a friend than a husband. Then I introduce you to Phillip Hamilton, one of the most eligible men in Atlanta, and you blow him off."

"I didn't blow him off. He's not interested in me. And I'm certainly not interested in him."

"What you gonna do, fix him up with Sharon like you did LeMar?"

"I told you I was, he'd be perfect for Sharon. And yes, I plan on introducing them at the party after the open house."

"You know, the only man I've ever seen you really excited about was LeMar. He showed up and you flipped out. I think you were happy to see him, you just wouldn't admit it."

"Look, you and Tony might be back together, but leave me alone. I'm not afraid of anything or anybody. And I don't want to talk about LeMar." She finished her lunch and got up from the table.

"I think I'll invite him to our little party," Doreece teased.

Rosie turned and glared at her sister. "Don't you dare."

Fifteen

As soon as LeMar returned home, he was going to kick back and fall asleep on the couch. Tonight would be his first night in a while without Eddie coming in.

He opened the door and stepped inside. From the corner of his eye he saw a shadow move. He turned to find a man charging at him. LeMar let go of the doorknob and threw up his hands to protect himself.

He grabbed the burglar by the wrist. Something was in his hand, but LeMar couldn't tell what. He prayed it wasn't a gun. They wrestled back and forth. A glint of light flickered off the object. It was a knife. LeMar knocked the man's hand against the stair rail and the knife flew across the floor.

He had to get that knife. When he turned to run for it, he tripped over something in the middle of the floor. Eddie's suitcase lay wide open with his belongings scattered around the floor. The burglar reached for LeMar's leg and pulled him back. A swift kick to the man's head freed him. Again, he lunged for the knife.

Just as LeMar put his hands on the handle, another hand gripped his. As they wrestled, LeMar felt the cold blade against his skin, then a strong stinging sensation. He released his grip. He rolled over grabbing his hand. The burglar stood across from him, holding out the knife ready to attack.

LeMar jumped to his feet. The burglar had a ski mask pulled over his face, preventing LeMar from seeing him.

"What the hell do you want?" LeMar demanded.

The burglar's only response was to wave his knife around.

Suddenly, another man wearing a mask came running down the stairs. LeMar's stomach churned, and he hoped the situation wasn't about to take a turn for the worse. He swung at the man in front of him, hitting him across the jaw. His punch landed, but simultaneously he felt a sharp pain in his side. He'd been stabbed.

The man who ran down the stairs continued out the front door. He called back at the other guy, "Come on, forget about him."

LeMar held one hand against his side and reached for one of the walking sticks at the bottom of the stairs. When he turned around, the other burglar was running past him. He threw out his foot and tripped him. The burglar fell to his knees just inside the front door. LeMar jumped on his back. He raised his stick to clobber the guy, but a blow to his head stopped him.

Before hitting the ground, he saw another figure standing over him.

Eddie pulled up to LeMar's house and popped his trunk. He took a few minutes to clean it out so he could get some clothes inside. He'd lied to LeMar about having a place in Riverdale. His buddy needed his space, and so did he. He couldn't inconvenience

LeMar any longer. He'd have to find a hotel with weekly rates until he could work something out.

Whistling an R. Kelly tune that was on the radio, he strolled up the steps to the front door. His brows furrowed when he saw the front door ajar and no lights on inside. Something was wrong. He looked back at LeMar's car in the driveway. It looked okay. With one hand he pushed the door open wider and peeked inside.

"LeMar, you in there?" he called out from the porch, not sure if it was safe to go in. He heard what sounded like a moan, then kicked the door wide open.

"LeMar," he called out again. He stepped into the foyer, leaving the door open for light. Feeling around the wall, he remembered there was no wall switch. He had to cross the room to the table lamp. "LeMar." He kept calling out to his buddy as he reached for the lamp.

He flicked the light on. "Hey, what the hell happened?" LeMar lay on the floor behind the front door, struggling to raise himself. Eddie brought his hand to his mouth in a fist at the sight of LeMar's blood-soaked shirt.

"Hold on, man, don't move." Eddie didn't know what to do. He looked over at his suitcase and grabbed a wad of clothes. He shoved them under LeMar's head. "Relax while I call the police."

He grabbed the cordless phone from the den and dialed 911. He ran up to the room he had occupied and kicked the door open. The room had been ripped to shreds. He walked down the hall to one of the guest rooms and opened the door. The room hadn't been touched. He walked in and closed the door behind him.

Bent over in agony, LeMar felt his head throb.

Holding one hand over his side, he pushed up on his elbow. Blood ran down his other hand from the wound. He grabbed one of Eddie's shirts and wrapped it around his hand as best he could. He pushed himself up until his back rested against the wall.

The pain in his side was worsening. He unzipped his jacket and raised his T-shirt. The sight of the gash made him flinch. He needed to get to a hospital.

Eddie came running back down the stairs. "I called the police and an ambulance, hang in there, dude." He kneeled down beside LeMar. "Did you get shot?"

"No, he had a knife." The words came out in a grunt.

"Did you see him?"

LeMar shook his head, lowered his T-shirt, and placed his hand back over the wound.

Eddie grabbed another shirt. "Here, press this against yourself to stop the bleeding." He looked over at his suitcase lying on the floor. Everything had been ripped out and thrown all over the room. He picked everything up and placed it back in the suitcase.

LeMar closed his eyes and tried to rest until the ambulance arrived.

When LeMar opened his eyes again, he was in the hospital. The doctors dressed his wounds, and the police were waiting outside.

"Mr. Reed, you're a very lucky man. I hope you realize that."

LeMar looked down at the bandage on his side and around his hand. "Yeah, I know."

"You could have been killed."

He looked up into the nurse's plump little face.

She was right. There were two men and if they'd wanted to, they could have killed him. Why hadn't they?

"Do you have any children, Mr. Reed?"

"No."

"You married?"

"Nope. I haven't had the pleasure yet."

"Well, that's the first time I've heard it put like that. Nevertheless I bet there's a young lady out there who would have been devastated had this been fatal."

Yeah, my mother. LeMar nodded. "Yeah, you're right. I'll try my best to make sure I don't run into any more knives. Or vice versa." He smiled at her so she would know he was joking.

Rosie had come to mind, but he didn't know how much she would care, if at all. Did she feel anything at all for him? He still had strong feelings for her. He didn't want to leave this earth without seeing if there could possibly ever be anything between them again. What they had so many years ago was special. He'd never had a relationship that special with anyone since.

"After you take these painkillers, I'm going to step out and let that policeman come in and talk with you. He has a few questions."

LeMar took the pills as the officer walked in. He was thankful it wasn't the same cop who'd shown up for the first break-in. He recalled as many details about his run-in with the burglars.

After the officer left, LeMar was released to go home. A nurse informed him that his friend was asleep in the waiting room. She offered to wake him and have him pull the car around. LeMar was a little unsteady on his feet. He walked out to the car with the nurse's help.

Eddie drove over a small bump in the road, causing LeMar to curse and grunt. "Man, take it easy."

"I'm sorry. How many stitches did you get?" Eddie asked.

LeMar gave him a snarl. "I don't know, I didn't count." Pain brought out the worst in him.

Eddie snorted. "That was a crazy question, sorry. How you feeling?"

What possessed him to ask such ridiculous questions? Le-Mar laid his head back on the headrest and closed his eyes. "I don't feel like talking. Just take me home."

They rode on in silence.

When they reached LeMar's house, Eddie helped him inside. LeMar gritted his teeth as they climbed the steps to his front porch.

"Man, didn't they give you any pain pills at the hospital?"

"Yeah, but they didn't kill all the pain."

Once inside, Eddie helped him out of his shirt. "What you want to do with this?" He held up the T-shirt.

"Throw it in the garbage can. I don't need a souvenir. You'll find some clean shirts in my top drawer."

LeMar stretched out on the couch while Eddie ran to get a shirt. Thank goodness Eddie had shown up. Then again, maybe if he hadn't, this never would have happened. As his suspicions about Eddie grew, Eddie walked into the room.

"Here." He handed LeMar a T-shirt. "You feel like taking a look around?"

"Just tell me if my computer's upstairs or not."

"It's still there. I checked when I called the police."

LeMar gave Eddie a long, searching look. "If they didn't take the computer, then what did they take?"

Eddie shrugged. "Nothing that I can tell. I talked to the policeman at the hospital. He wants you to have a look around and let him know if anything's missing. Here's his card." Eddie took the card from his pocket and laid it on the table.

LeMar laid his head back on a pillow and let out a long sigh.

"You think you can make it upstairs?"

"If I wanted to, but I don't. I'm crashing right here." He looked up. "What time is it, anyway?"

Eddie looked at his watch. "It's almost four o'clock in the morning."

"I'm fine right here. Is the lock broken on the door?"

"I'll check it out and make sure everything's locked up. I'll hang out down here with you tonight, in case those guys come back."

After securing the back door and making sure everything else was locked up, Eddie returned to the den. LeMar was fast asleep. He took a seat in the recliner and turned on the television. He pulled a small gun from his jacket pocket and set it in his lap.

They spent the night in the den.

LeMar woke the next morning in pain. He stood slowly and went to take the pain pills he found in his jacket pocket. In the kitchen he saw how Eddie had propped a kitchen chair under the doorknob. Now LeMar was ready to purchase that alarm system. He made a mental note to call someone later in the day.

He shuffled back into the den. Eddie was still asleep in the recliner. LeMar moved to turn away, but saw something out of the corner of his eye. He turned back to Eddie. There was a gun in his lap. LeMar hated guns.

He sat down on the couch again and studied his friend. Why on earth would he need to carry a gun, unless he was expecting trouble? He contemplated how to wake him. He didn't want to startle him, not with a gun so close at hand.

He walked over and quickly lifted the gun from Eddie's lap. Looking around for a safe place to put it, he chose the drawer under the television. Then he shook Eddie to wake him up. As LeMar suspected he would, Eddie jumped up, reaching for the gun.

When he looked up and saw LeMar, he cursed, realizing what he'd done. "What did you do with my gun?" he demanded.

"I put it away. I didn't want to take a chance on either one of us getting shot." He walked back over to the couch and eased down.

"What the hell do you need a gun for anyway? Talk to me this morning. I want to know what's going on."

Eddie gave him a baffled look. "Nothing's going on. What you talking about?"

"Man, I've never known you to own a gun before. And you know I don't like them, but you bring one into my house. What's up?"

"A man's gotta protect himself."

"From what, or whom?"

Eddie lowered his head, then looked up slowly. "We don't exactly run in the same circles, in case you haven't noticed. From time to time, I have to watch my back. Besides, those guys might come back."

"Did it ever dawn on you that if you weren't doing things like running illegal card games you wouldn't have to watch your back?"

"I do what I have to do." Eddie jumped up in a huff. "Sorry. I don't have a master's degree and no fancy job like you."

"We're not talking about me. Stop looking for a cop-out all the time."

"Oh, I didn't have the help you had to get through school, so I'm copping out. Guess I just haven't been as lucky as you," he said sarcastically.

"Man, don't give me that. Both of us had grants. I didn't have any more help than you did. I even offered to help you—"

"I didn't need your help then, and I don't need it now. You always lucked out in school and got the right classes, the right jobs, the right everything. Then, like a fool, I helped you get the right girl."

"What do you mean, you helped me?" LeMar was taken aback by that one.

"I introduced you to Rosie, and you knew damned well I was interested in her. She should have been my girl, not yours," he said, pointing at LeMar.

"Man, not once did you act like you were interested in her."

"Yeah, well, I didn't have a chance to get to know her before you guys started knocking boots."

"What are you talking about? You knew her before I did."

"Yeah, and I know stuff about—" He stared at LeMar, shaking his head. "Man, she's just not the perfect little angel you think she is."

LeMar had to laugh. "Eddie, come on, let's stop this. I don't want to argue with you about Rosie. I want to know who broke into my house."

"So what you saying? I had something to do with what happened here last night, too? You already blame me for the first break-in."

Now it was LeMar's time to stand up. He struggled.

"Yes, I think you know what they were looking for. Come on, man, the policeman at the hospital told me how they ripped up that room upstairs. They were searching for something, and I want to know what."

Eddie stormed out of the den. "I'm outta here." He hesitated in the hallway.

LeMar watched him, knowing something was on his mind. "Come on, Eddie, quit being stubborn and let me help you."

"I told you I had nothing to do with it. I'll come back tonight for the rest of my things."

Sixteen

Rosie pulled up to LeMar's house, not expecting to see his car at ten-thirty in the morning. But that was better than seeing Eddie's car. She hadn't seen him lately, and hoped he was gone for good.

She carried a six-foot artificial ficus tree up the steps with her. After three rings of the doorbell LeMar hadn't come to the door, so she opened it with her key. As she stepped inside, she heard a beep. She looked around and saw a panel on the wall. He'd installed an alarm system. Thank God it wasn't armed. She set the tree down and called out, not wanting to catch him at a bad time.

"LeMar, it's Rosie. I rang the bell, but you didn't answer," she called out.

"Hey, come on in."

He stood at the top of the stairs looking down at her. Suddenly, it dawned on her that he might have company. Was she in the way today? "I'm sorry, did I show up at a bad time?"

"No, you're fine. I couldn't make it to the door fast enough."

"Well, I have a few more plants in the car. I'll be right back." She walked out the door thinking that he could offer to help. He'd been giving her the cold shoulder too much lately. She grabbed two small artificial arrangements from the trunk and went back inside.

LeMar was standing midway down the stairs. Something was wrong, she sensed it. She set the plants by the tree and walked over to the foot of the stairs. "Are you okay?"

"Yeah. I had another break-in a few days ago." He continued down the stairs.

"You're kidding! My God, two break-ins in one month, that's crazy."

"I know. As you see, I installed an alarm system." He pointed at the panel on the wall.

"I didn't know this area was that bad. What did they take this time?"

"Nothing. I think the same guys came back because they were looking for something."

"Eddie." That's all she said.

He shook his head. "I think he had something to do with it. He denies it, but I think he's in some type of trouble."

"LeMar, he stays in trouble. I saw him a couple of weeks ago at Café 290 with some thug-looking guys. They looked like they were about to rob the place. Is he still staying here?"

"No, he moved out. He said he's got a job and everything."

"Sounds like you don't believe him."

He shook his head and walked toward the kitchen. "I'm not sure what to believe anymore. Everywhere I turn, people keep lying to me." He peered back over his shoulder at her.

She averted her eyes to the floor. Her heart raced. She could see in his eyes that he knew something, but how much did he know? "I wouldn't trust anything Eddie says." She turned back to her artificial plants. "Well, I need to set these around."

"When you finish, come in the kitchen a minute. I'd like to speak to you."

"Sure." Her hands trembled as she took the tree into the dining room and positioned it close to the window. The other plants went into his new office down the hall. She moved the plants from one spot to another. She needed to stall.

She didn't want to go into that kitchen. LeMar's playful flirting had stopped weeks ago. He was more serious and direct with her now, and she didn't like it. Unable to stall any longer, she went into the kitchen. He held on to the table to sit down; his face twisted in pain.

"Are you all right?" she asked, deeply concerned.

He let out a long sigh after he sat down. "I interrupted the burglars who broke in, and got cut."

She rushed over and stood next to him. "You mean you fought with them?"

"Yeah." He sipped his coffee.

She sat on the edge of the chair next to him. "LeMar, that's crazy, you could have been killed."

He looked into her eyes. "I know. I'm lucky to be alive."

"How bad is it?" She reached out, wanting to touch him. After holding her hand awkwardly in mid-air, she pulled it back.

"Only a couple of stitches, it's not too bad." He raised his shirt and showed her the bandage.

Her lips formed a mute *O* before she held a hand over her mouth. The bandage was big and wrapped around his side. She sat back in her seat and took a deep breath.

"Rosie, why did you lie to me?" He couldn't avoid the issue any longer. Her eyes widened innocently like she didn't know what he was talking about. But he knew better.

"I know you've been divorced for more than two years." He bit his lip and searched her face for an answer.

She lowered her head. "Who told you?"

"It doesn't matter. I want to know why you felt like you had to lie." He pointed to himself, tapping his chest. "To me, of all people." His voice rose.

She scooted her chair back, distancing herself from him a bit. A sick feeling washed over her. "I'm sorry. I didn't want you to think you could walk back into my life after what you did to me."

He ran a hand across his forehead. "After what I did to you? How about what you did to me? I went back to handle family business, and you up and got married on me."

"LeMar, I knew about your new girlfriend in D.C."

"What girlfriend? I wasn't seeing anybody. You just couldn't wait until I got myself straight."

Now she raised her voice. "I had a friend who told me all about Monica, the redhead. Remember her?"

"Monica." He laughed. "I don't believe this. Monica's an old high-school friend. That's all. I never even went out with her. Is that why you up and married some guy? You thought I was seeing Monica?"

"No, of course not." How could she explain her and David's sudden relationship?

"What did he do, get you pregnant or something?"

"No." *You did.* "I can't explain it. We were good friends."

"And that's why you married him?" He raised his voice again.

"No. Quit hollering at me. I don't have to explain anything to you. Besides, your cousin Mary told me you were out with your girlfriend when I called. Why would she lie to me?"

"Mary! Don't tell me you believed her? Rosie, she's

got about as much sense as Eddie has. She's good at keeping stuff going, that's all." He rested his forehead in his palm. "I can't believe you even listened to her."

"I spent weeks trying to get in touch with you before you finally called. Then I'm supposed to be your Atlanta girlfriend while you've got a new D.C. girlfriend? I don't think so."

"You totally misunderstood. My mother was devastated, so that left me to settle my father's business. Don't you understand I'm an only child? There wasn't anyone else to help. You should have been more patient."

"I was patient."

"Like hell you were. I had to track you down three months later to find out you'd gotten married. Your husband answered the phone. Imagine my surprise."

She was surprised. "You called my house?" she asked with a shaky voice.

"Yeah. What a way to find out that my girl was married." He scratched his head, then ran his hand over his face in a frustrated manner. "This is ridiculous. Look, we can't change the past, but we don't have to let it ruin the future. You didn't have to lie to me. That's all I wanted to say."

She wanted to tell him about the baby so badly, but she couldn't bring herself to do it.

"No more lies, okay?" He waited for her to agree.

She gazed at him, knowing that not telling him about the baby was like lying to him. *God forgive me.*

She finally agreed. "No more. So, who told you I was divorced?"

LeMar smiled at her. "That's not fair. I promised not to tell."

She felt all the tension leave the air. "Okay, that's

good enough. I think I know who told you." She sat there nodding her head.

"Take it easy on her, I like her." LeMar slowly got up.

"Oh, I love her to death, but she talks too much, especially to strangers. She didn't even know you, and she told you all my business."

"She said you've been talking about me." He placed his coffee cup in the dishwasher, grunting as he bent over.

"Here, let me get that." Rosie rushed over, took the cup from him, and placed it in the dishwasher.

"You been talking about me?" LeMar asked, standing over her.

She closed the dishwasher and stood. "I told her about your house, that's all."

"She's fond of you, I can tell."

"Yeah, we're big buddies." She walked over to the table and picked up her purse.

"I gathered as much. You know, we used to be big buddies like that, too. Do you think we'll ever be reunited?"

"Not like we used to be. I can't go backwards, Le-Mar. So much has happened in my life over the past twelve years. I've got to keep moving forward. That's why I did what I did."

"Uh, yeah." He felt as if he'd been stabbed again.

"Well, if you're finished, I've gotta run. Do you need anything before I go?"

"No, but thanks for asking."

"If you think of something you need"—she turned before walking out the kitchen—"just give me a call."

He stood there, gripping the back of a chair. "Sure."

Rosie left feeling as if a boulder had been lifted

from her shoulders. Everything was out in the open now. Well, almost everything.

The Colony House was complete and the open-house ceremony was under way. Rosie conducted the first walk-through with the builder and the new home-owner. Looking over at the mother and her three children, Rosie felt really good. The little girls were so beautiful, she hoped they'd like their rooms. She remembered having to share her room with Doreece and hating it most of her teenage years. These little girls would each have their own room. She hoped they realized how blessed they were.

As they entered the house, the mother started crying. The girls ran to their rooms, then Rosie started crying. She wouldn't give up anything for being able to give of herself and her talent in this way.

After the walk-through, she looked around for Carrie, but didn't see her. She didn't know whether to be concerned or not. Doreece had taken care of getting her there.

"Sis, I'm proud to have helped you with this one." Doreece elbowed Rosie as she wiped her eyes.

"Thank you. I guess I can count on you next year, too, right?"

"You bet. This can be our project, something we do together. I think I'd like that."

"Doreece, I won't be able to find you next year when I start clawing for sponsors." Rosie laughed.

"Yes, you will, you'll see. I brought you him, didn't I?" She pointed to Phillip Hamilton, who'd already introduced himself to Sharon.

"Yes, you did. Look, I don't have to try and fix him up with Sharon after all."

"No, honey, she already took care of that. I saw

her inching her way over to him earlier. And I think
you're right about them."

"What's that?"

"They do make a good couple. She looks good on
his arm, and I'm sure she loves being there."

"At least she'll enjoy the ride. Not like when I set
her up with LeMar. He bored her to death."

"Why did you do that?"

Rosie shrugged. "I thought they'd look good together."

"Girl, you're something else, you know that? It
sounds like some of Mrs. Carrie is rubbing off on
you. Setting people up."

"Speaking of—where is she? I thought you were
going to pick her up?"

"Uh, I was, but she had a ride already."

"Who's she riding with?" Rosie asked, surprised.

"She said she's bringing a friend, so I gave her
directions. It's probably one of her lady friends."

"Which one? Her lady friends don't drive."

"I don't know, but don't worry about her, she'll
be here."

"Sorry, I'm running a little late." LeMar held out
his arm for Carrie as she stepped out her front door.

"Don't worry about it, honey." She waved her
hand at him. "We'll get there, that's all that matters.
I just want to see that house. We don't have to be
the first to arrive."

LeMar helped her out into the car.

"I'm just glad you could pick me up. I didn't want
Rosie to have to come back on this side of town to
get me when she needed to be there so early."

"Are you sure she'll be okay if I show up?"

"I'm positive. You're my guest. Now remember

what I told you. She needs a man in her life, she's just stubborn."

"I don't know, she made it pretty clear a couple of days ago that she didn't want to get involved with me again."

"Young man, do you still love her?" she asked in a feisty tone.

"Yes, ma'am, more than anything."

"Then trust me on this one. After the ceremony, we'll have dinner. Then you kids can go out dancing. As usual, everyone will have a date except her. I'm usually her date." She gave a soft little laugh.

"What's so funny?"

"I bet she's driving herself crazy wondering who to wait on since I'm not there."

Rosie personally thanked each of the sponsors and invited them to the small celebration afterward. She took pictures with the developers and tried not to follow the cocktail tray around. Those little bites were her first meal of the day. She was starved and ready for dinner.

As she conversed with Neville and one of her furniture store sponsors, she spotted Carrie out of the corner of her eye. She exhaled deeply. Now she could relax. Or so she thought.

As Carrie crossed the floor, Rosie saw a man behind her and almost choked on her cocktail. LeMar was with her. What was he doing there? He looked in Rosie's direction and their eyes locked. At that moment, she knew she was in trouble. They came closer, and she excused herself, walking in the opposite direction.

"Rosie, Rosie," Carrie called out to her.

She couldn't ignore her. She stopped and spun

around. "Oh, I see you made it. I was getting worried. I didn't know how you were getting here." She looked up at LeMar.

"I hope you don't mind me being here. Mrs. Carrie invited me." LeMar grinned.

Before she could answer, Carrie grabbed her by the arm. "Honey, this is the cutest little house I've ever seen. Why don't you show us around." She pulled Rosie toward the living room.

Rosie looked back at LeMar, who shrugged and smiled. He followed as she gave them the grand tour.

After a while, she pulled Carrie aside. "You know, I should be mad at you," Rosie scolded her as she showed off the house.

"What for?"

Rosie stopped and gave her neighbor a don't-even-try-it look. Then she lowered her voice. "You betrayed me, for one thing. Since when had you and LeMar become such good friends?"

"Honey, I never betrayed you. I did you a favor, you just don't know it yet." She tugged on Rosie's arm. "Now, come on and show me those angels you talked about."

LeMar had bumped into one of the developers and stopped to talk.

As the ceremony wound down, Rosie made sure everyone had her business card. Doreece checked that brochures were placed around the house and she was available to book appointments if anyone wanted one.

Carrie positioned herself near the cocktail table, bending the ear of one of the sponsor's wives.

"So, you're not upset with me, are you?"

Rosie turned to find LeMar standing behind her. She felt his breath against her ear. Her body shivered as she caught her breath and contemplated what to say.

"I shouldn't have come," he declared when she didn't respond.

"No, it's okay, really. This is a private party. Besides, you get to see what else I can do. My specialty is African design, but I'm not too bad at American contemporary either."

"It's nice. What I can't believe is that you did the whole house for less than ten thousand dollars. That's unbelievable."

Her stomach growled. She was sure he heard it. She took a deep breath and held her hand to her stomach. She tried to talk over it. "A lot of people volunteered their time to make that happen."

"Are you hungry?" He laughed at the sight of her sucking in her stomach.

She laughed as well, and let out a deep breath. "I'm starving. I can't wait to get out of here and eat. I haven't had anything today but those little hors d'oeuvres. And I didn't want to eat them all up, although I could have."

Doreece walked over and joined them. "So, I'm not the only one who's hungry. I hear you two talking food."

"Rosie's stomach is over here shouting at her." He laughed and extended his hand. "It's good to see you again, Doreece."

"Nice to see you, too. Are you coming to dinner with us?"

Rosie froze. She could have kicked Doreece.

LeMar looked around for Carrie, "I'm not sure what my date has planned for tonight."

Doreece laughed. "Your date, that's cute. I'm sure she'd love to come with us. I'm surprised Rosie hasn't already invited you." She turned to look at her sister.

"Yeah, uh . . ." Her voice croaked, and she cleared her throat. "We're going to Justin's after we leave here. You're welcome to join us." She smiled at him but hoped he'd say no.

"I'd love to." He accepted the invitation with a broad smile.

How come I knew he'd say that? She stood there holding her stomach and her heart.

Seventeen

The dinner crowd was smaller. The Colony Homes team and Rosie's team were the only ones invited. They celebrated another successful year. Throughout her meal, Rosie glanced up and saw LeMar engaged in conversation with Tony. Every time he laughed, she found herself smiling. She'd always been attracted to his robust laughter, which brightened his whole face. She just hated to admit it. She couldn't allow herself to fall in love with him again. She wouldn't allow it.

After dinner, the crowd left for Club Taste, the spot for the afterparty. She said good night to Carrie and gave her a kiss on the cheek.

"Honey, I'm so proud of you. That house was beautiful, and the family appreciated it so much. You do good work." She grabbed Rosie by the arms and gave her a big hug. Pulling back, she kissed her on the cheek. "Now go have some fun."

"Thank you, Mrs. Carrie. I'm riding with Doreece and Tony tonight. Are you going to be all right?"

"Of course I am. This young man is taking me home." She held her hand out for LeMar, who was approaching.

"What, my date's ready to go home so early? You mean you're not going to party with us?"

With us! Rosie's lips parted as she stared up at him.

"No, honey, I can't keep up with you young folks. It's past my bedtime. But I want you two to have a good time tonight."

"Rosie, come on," Doreece called from Tony's waiting car.

She turned back around as LeMar helped Carrie into the car. He closed the door and turned to Rosie. "Looks like I'll see you later."

He gave her a rather seductive grin before getting into the car. She watched them pull off as she walked over to Tony's car. Getting in, she slammed the door.

"Hey, watch the door," Tony called out.

Doreece turned and looked innocently at her sister. "What's wrong?"

"You did this, didn't you?" Rosie narrowed her eyes.

"Did what?"

"Invited him. He's coming to the club." She crossed her arms and looked out the window.

"No, I didn't invite him, but I'm glad he's coming. I like him."

"So, he invited himself?" she asked sarcastically.

"I invited him," Tony admitted. "He seems like a pretty cool dude. Nothing to be afraid of."

Rosie slammed her fist into the seat and grunted. "For the last time, I am not afraid of men. And I don't care what you guys think."

Tony observed her through his rearview mirror. "Uh-huh."

She sat with her arms folded in silence as they continued to the club. Tony and Doreece talked, but Rosie never commented. She pretended not to hear them as she looked out the window.

Tonight she wanted to cut loose and enjoy herself. She wanted to mingle and flirt, something she rarely did. She couldn't do any of that with LeMar there. He made her nervous and uncomfortable most of the time. She didn't like the way he looked at her. He didn't merely look, he stared. Her night would be ruined.

On her second glass of wine, Rosie was in the mood for fun. She hadn't spotted LeMar. Perhaps he'd changed his mind. If he didn't come because of the way she'd looked at him, she'd feel bad. She didn't want him to feel unwelcome. She wanted him to have something better to do. At least, that's what she told herself every time she looked toward the entrance.

"Here she is. The lady of the hour."

Rosie turned to see Neville and his partner, Roy, holding up their glasses to salute her. "Oh, thank you." She slid off her stool and leaned over to kiss Neville on the cheek.

He gave her a one-arm hug and kiss. "We need a toast."

She grabbed her glass and held it up. "Here, here."

"To my boss. The best damned interior designer in Atlanta." They tapped glasses, then raised them.

"Rosie, I love what you did with that place. Neville took me by there earlier to see the before picture. And I can't believe how stunning it looks. I'm jealous of that family. I'd live there any day."

"Thanks Roy, that's so sweet of you."

"You know, this is nice of Colony Homes to throw this little shindig. After we finish Mr. Man's house, we'll have to have our own little party."

"You mean Mr. Reed's house," she said in a proper tone, with her chin and glass lifted.

"The one and only." Neville followed her tone.

"Yes, darling, we'll throw a posh little soiree, inviting only the best people. And I know the perfect spot. Castle LeRosie's."

They joined her in laughter. "Hey, it's within the budget," she continued.

"Speaking of our number one client"—Neville cleared his throat—"he's headed this way."

Rosie's stomach turned into one big knot. She licked her lips and swallowed the large lump in her throat. Suddenly, she didn't know what to do with her hands.

"Hello, Neville." LeMar joined their little circle.

"Hey, Mr. Reed, good to see you." Neville introduced Roy, and they exchanged greetings.

LeMar turned to Rosie, clasping his hands together. "Mrs. Wright, what would it take to get you on the dance floor?"

An act of God was the first thing that came to mind. *Why am I being so mean to him?* This was her night, and she hadn't planned on spending it with him, that was the problem.

When she didn't answer, he held his hands out, pleading. "What do you say?"

What the hell, she told herself. He'd already messed up her night by being here. She set what was left of her drink on the table. "Let's dance." She waved to Neville and Roy.

LeMar's eyebrows shot up as he grinned and took her hand. He led the way to the dance floor.

They danced through several songs. Rosie sang along with the music and realized it was "Fantasy" by Mariah Carey. The words seemed to match what she was feeling at the moment. She used to dream of LeMar coming back for her and the two of them starting all over. That was, until she'd given up on him and moved on with her life.

The DJ slowed the tempo down. Several people left the floor. Rosie turned to walk away, but LeMar reached out and grabbed her by the waist.

She turned around and looked up at him. He shook his head. "Uh-uh. You're not getting away from me that easy."

He gently pulled her into his arms and closed the distance between them. She opened her mouth to protest, but her body screamed yes. She stiffened as his hands glided along her back.

He whispered into her ear, "Relax."

The heat from his mouth warmed her entire body. She had the urge to lay her head against his chest, but pulled back instead.

She cleared her throat. "LeMar, I'm not a great slow dancer, maybe we—"

"Yes, you are. Just place your arms around me and close your eyes." He wrapped his arms around her and pulled her back into his embrace. "It'll all come back to you," he whispered.

Biting her lip, she melted right into his arms. She inhaled the clean smell of his cologne and felt the seductive way he moved against her. Her body responded to every dip, swerve, and grind.

This reminded her of a Friday night fraternity dance down at the Bottom, a local hole-in-the-wall that the students loved. LeMar would hold her close and kiss her neck while they danced to a Luther Vandross tune. For two college students, that was foreplay. Their bodies would become one as they grooved as close to ecstasy as they could with their clothes on. Sometimes they'd capped off the evening with LeMar sneaking into Rosie's dorm room for the night.

That same heat was present tonight. As the song

came to an end, she felt the soft touch of his lips against her cheek.

"Thank you," he said, barely above a whisper, as he pulled away.

She uncurled her toes and smoothed out her dress. "You're welcome." She struggled to control the quavering of her voice.

He placed a hand on the small of her back and led her off the dance floor. An entire area of the club was sectioned off for their party. There were more than enough seats for everyone and plenty of food. As they stepped up into the section, Doreece and Tony walked up behind them.

Rosie quickly turned around to LeMar. "Excuse me, I need to run to the ladies' room." She made her way through the crowd and into the ladies' room. Luckily, it was empty. She grabbed a paper towel and ran some water over it. Looking in the mirror, she patted her face down. *My God, what am I doing?* She'd managed to groove her way back into the past. She'd held that man like she wanted to have sex with him, but she didn't, did she?

"No, no, no," she chastised herself. She ran the towel under the cold water again.

When she returned to the table, Sharon came and sat next to her. "We're getting ready to cut out of here. Phillip wants to stop by the Martini Club for a few minutes."

Rosie smiled triumphantly. "And I didn't even have to introduce you."

Sharon licked her lips and lowered her head, smiling. "I guess you could say I don't like to waste time. There's no shame in my game. I had to meet that man."

Rosie laughed. "Friend, I ain't mad at ya."

"And"—Sharon scooted her chair closer to Rosie—

"who was that I saw you on the dance floor with a few minutes ago? Your old college friend." Sharon gave her a lopsided grin.

Rosie rested her elbow on the table and placed her head in her hand. "I don't know what I'm doing."

"You're enjoying yourself. And you guys were out there grinding the hell out of that song. Girl, I'm proud of you." She elbowed Rosie. "I didn't know you had it in you."

Now Rosie wanted to crawl under the table. "God, was it that bad?"

"Rosie, it's me. Don't pretend you don't like the guy when I know you do. When we went out, he must have asked me more than a dozen questions about you."

Rosie sat back and crossed her arms. She could see LeMar standing at the end of the long table. He had a drink in his hand and was talking with one of her sponsors. He must have felt her eyes on him, because he looked right at her, saying more than words ever could.

She hadn't cooled off from the dance, and now he was making her hotter.

"I know you guys had something special, and I want to hear all about it." She stood. "I'm going to call you tomorrow, and I want the whole story. Then explain why you didn't tell me before."

They said good night, and Rosie went to get herself another drink. No matter where she stood in the room, every time she looked up, LeMar was standing in her direct view.

Every time she sat down, she could smell his cologne and feel his hands on the small of her back. She needed to go home.

She finally located Doreece and Tony and asked if they were ready to go. "Come on, Rosie, the night's still young. You can't be ready to go home," Doreece pleaded.

"I've had a long day. And if you don't stay off your feet, your ankles will swell. I knew I should have driven my own car."

"Just a few more dances, and we'll be ready to leave." Doreece grabbed Tony's hand and led him to the dance floor again.

Rosie sat watching them.

"Had about enough?" came a voice from behind her.

She shook her head, knowing it was LeMar. He'd watched her all night. She looked up as he stepped around in front of her and grabbed a seat.

"Yeah, I'm ready to call it quits. I've been up since six this morning."

He shook his head. "Yeah, me too." He looked out at the dance floor, then back at Rosie. "I can walk you to your car when you're ready to go."

"I didn't drive. Doreece and Tony will drop me off." She pointed at the dance floor.

They were in the middle of a "party over here" chant. "I don't think they'll be ready anytime soon." LeMar gave Rosie a raised-brow grin. "I can take you, it's no problem."

"You're just a regular taxi tonight, aren't you?" she said.

"Looks that way, but don't worry, the meter's not running." He stood to help her up. "Reed's Taxi at your service."

She eyed him skeptically, before realizing he was her only way home unless she wanted to wait until Doreece and Tony ran out of gas.

On the way out, she motioned to Doreece that LeMar was taking her home. Doreece waved back and smiled at her. Rosie rolled her eyes.

LeMar opened the car door and held her hand as she climbed in. Tonight she didn't have on her wedding ring. The day he returned it, she'd put it away.

Smooth jazz music filled the car after LeMar started the engine. She eased out of her shoes and laid her head back on the headrest. "I'm exhausted."

"Funny, you don't look it."

She turned and gave him an are-you-kidding look, and noticed the sexy grin on his face. In the night light with jazz music setting the scene, he looked so sexy. She bit her lip and closed her eyes. "Thank you, but I am."

They chatted about the house, music, Sharon and Phillip, even Carrie. By the time they reached Rosie's house, they were enjoying themselves. LeMar pulled up in front of the house, but kept the motor running.

"I've got an idea. Let's run down to the Varsity for a milk shake and some fries."

Rosie looked out the window at Carrie's house. "I really should check on Mrs. Carrie."

"Do you think she's still up?" he asked, looking at his watch. "It's after one o'clock in the morning."

"No, you're right, she's probably asleep." Now she had no excuse. And he knew she loved the Varsity's milk shakes. She looked at LeMar, thinking she was headed for trouble.

"The Varsity," they said at the same time.

He pulled off and headed downtown. The Varsity was packed. There weren't any spots at the drive-up stations, but they were lucky to find a parking spot in the front lot. "I wonder what's going on tonight," she said.

"I don't know, but there must be a ball game somewhere that just let out. I'll go grab our food and be right back. Want our old favorite?"

She nodded. "You remember?"

"Of course," he said, climbing out of the car. He ordered the same thing he would have gotten twelve years ago, two large orders of fries and two strawberry shakes. Shakes so thick you almost needed a spoon.

When he returned, they started to eat in the car. Then Rosie slurped up a little too much, and the top popped off, sending milk shake down her dress.

"Oh, man, look at me!" She felt the cold drink as it penetrated through the material.

LeMar grabbed the few napkins he'd brought out and gave them to her. He took her shake while she opened up the car door and jumped out. She tried to knock the leftover milk shake off her lap. It ran down her new dress, creating a mess.

After dabbing at what she could, she got back into the car. "Man, this is gonna stain, and I won't be able to get it out."

"Yes, you will. Come on, we'll run over to my place real quick." He started the car and hurried to his house about five minutes away.

Once inside, Rosie went straight into the bathroom and took off her dress. With a washcloth and some water, she made an attempt to get out the stain. Creating a bigger wet spot than before, she put the dress back on and walked into the den.

LeMar had turned on the music and the television at the same time, but muted the television. He rose from the couch when she walked into the room.

Rosie chuckled, looking down at herself, then up at him. "You know, you always stand up when I walk into the room."

He shrugged. "That's what my mother taught me

to do when I see a lady. Come here." He pointed at
the food on the coffee table.

She walked over to the couch. "Well, I'll have to
carry this to the cleaners tomorrow, but it looks like
I saved the dress."

"Look at it this way, at least you're not as wet as
the day you showed up to work." They sat down and
laughed together.

"Oh, that was a mess. I was so embarrassed. And
it hasn't rained that hard since then."

Rosie watched television while she finished off her
milk shake and fries. LeMar had finished his. She
kept asking herself what she was doing there at one
o'clock in the morning. She needed to finish her
food and leave. Her dress could have waited until
they'd reached her house.

They watched a few videos in silence, then commented on how they had changed over the years.
Were they getting older, or was everything getting sex-
ier? The lines between porn and sexy were getting
blurred.

When a slow tune came on, LeMar stood up, grabbing Rosie's hand. "Come here, dance with me."

"LeMar, the party's over, and I should be going
home," she protested while standing.

He walked around the coffee table, still holding
her hand, until he stood in front of her. "The party's
not over yet."

Eighteen

They exchanged scorching looks as she walked into his outstretched arms. Her body ached from a burning desire to feel his hands all over her. She wanted him to touch her the way he used to, to explore every inch of her, and then some.

"You know, I was glad to see you still lived here when I bumped into you. I think about you a lot."

"LeMar, after you left, I quit school."

He stopped dancing and looked down into her eyes.

"It took me more than a year to return and finish my degree. Then, after my marriage didn't work out, I started my own business." She hadn't intended to confess so much, but couldn't stop herself.

"I don't know what you and David had, but I know what you and I had was special. I was lying in the hospital a couple of days ago thinking about how I needed to share my feelings with you. If I left this earth and didn't tell you that I still loved you, I'd never forgive myself."

When she looked up into his smoldering hazel eyes, she knew she wouldn't be able to hold back any longer. He'd taken all his cards out and laid them on the table. Now she had to respond.

"I went through some things after you left, that I

don't know if I'll ever be able to talk to you about. You broke my heart."

"Your heart wasn't the only one broken. I'm sorry that I lost you." He placed a small kiss on her forehead. "But, trust me, I wasn't trying to."

They held each other and danced. Rosie's body was on fire. She let out soft little moans each time LeMar kissed her on the neck or shoulder. His heart pounded so hard she felt it against her chest.

He suddenly stopped dancing and withdrew from her. Taking her face in his hands, he lifted her chin and kissed her deeply and passionately. If she'd had too much to drink earlier, it had worn off. She was fully aware of his tongue in her mouth, searching and probing every inch.

Her body responded in a way it hadn't in years. She relaxed her shoulders and reached out, pulling him closer to her. *God, don't let him stop.* When their bodies met, she felt his desire for her as strong as her own.

He stopped kissing her and tried to catch his breath. The sweet smell of her perfume and the clean scent of her hair intoxicated him. He hadn't planned to bring her here tonight. He hadn't planned anything actually, Carrie had. He was to escort her to the party in order to be with Rosie. However, after he danced with her, he couldn't walk away.

She put her hand on his chest as if she wanted to push him away. He took her hand into his and brought it to his mouth. He kissed her knuckles, then down the back of her hand and up her arm. Every time she moaned, he groaned inwardly. He had to have her.

He took her hand into his and walked out of the

den and toward the stairs. Standing at the foot of the stairs, he turned to look into her eyes. They widened as she held tightly to his hand.

"Tell me you want this as much as I do. I can't do it if you don't," he said eagerly.

She bit her lip and shook her head, "I do," she whispered nervously.

Together they climbed the stairs to his bedroom.

The next morning, Rosie stirred in bed, feeling the sheet against her body. She ran her hand down her side and realized she was naked. When she rolled over on her back, she remembered where she was.

"Hungry?" LeMar asked.

She turned to see him propped up on one elbow, gazing at her. She tried to hold back a blush, but was unsuccessful. She smiled all over the place.

"Is that a yes?"

"Yes, why? Are you cooking me breakfast?"

He leaned over and kissed her on the forehead. "Yes, ma'am, just tell me what you want. I'll even bring it up here."

"Wow, breakfast in bed. What did I do to you last night?"

"If you only knew." He kissed her again before climbing out of bed and finding his underwear across the room on the floor. He brought hers over and laid it at the foot of the bed.

"How does eggs and bacon sound?"

"Throw some pancakes in there and you've got a deal."

He smiled at her from the doorway. "My, my, you worked up an appetite, didn't you?"

She propped herself up on his pillows. "No, I'm just—" She stopped and smiled at him.

"You're always hungry after sex." He smiled back and winked at her. "I remember."

She looked around nervously. "What time is it? I bet Doreece is wondering what happened to me." She glanced around the room for a clock.

"Relax, she called this morning, and I told her you were okay."

She threw a hand over her mouth in shock. "How did she know to call here?"

"You left with me. Who else would she call? Don't worry, I assured her that you were being taken very, very good care of."

She looked at him, scared to respond, scared of what might come out of her mouth. What had happened to them last night? Did she really want him back, or was she responding to lust?

She threw a pillow at him. "Go fix my breakfast."

He laughed and threw the pillow back before going into the bathroom.

She heard him go down the stairs, whistling like a man satisfied. She sat there shaking her head, wondering if it was the wine she'd had earlier. Her body had reacted so naturally to his, and together they were perfect.

He was a part of her past, a client, everything with which she wasn't supposed to be getting involved. She'd broken all her rules last night. What had happened to her willpower?

Then there was the baby. She'd forgotten all about the baby for a moment. That was another reason this was no good. After last night, she had to tell him. Now wasn't a good time, but she'd have to eventually. While she waited for her breakfast, she lay back and rested.

* * *

LeMar put the bacon on first. He put some water on for coffee and went into the den to turn on the stereo. He was in such a good mood this morning. He had his Rosie back. They could start all over again and make it work this time. She wanted it as much as he did. He could see it in her eyes.

He heard a light tapping at the front door and went to see who it was. Eddie stood on the other side of the door with his hands in his pockets. LeMar cursed under his breath. Now was not a good time for Eddie to show up. He opened the door.

"Hey, man, I tried to catch you before you left to play ball. Can I talk to you a minute?"

LeMar held the door open. "Come on in." The last time they'd talked they'd argued, and he didn't feel like arguing with Eddie this morning. He didn't want him to know Rosie was there, either. "I'm not playing ball this morning, but I still don't have much time."

"I'll make it quick."

The whistle blew on the teakettle. Eddie followed LeMar into the kitchen. LeMar prepared himself a cup of coffee. "Want some?"

"No, thanks." Eddie sat down.

"What did you want to talk about?" LeMar needed him to say what he had to and leave.

"I wasn't exactly up front with you about some things the other day." He looked down and tapped his fingers against the table.

"What do you mean, you lied?"

He shook his head. "Kind of. I said I didn't know anything about who broke in here, but I think I do."

LeMar rested his elbow on the table and squeezed his bottom lip to keep from getting upset. "Let's have it."

"It may have been Dru Stone and one of his buddies."

"May have been? Was it or wasn't it?" he asked bluntly.

Eddie looked up at him. "I'm not sure. I haven't seen him in a couple of weeks, but I ran into a friend of his. She told me that he'd been looking for me and to watch my back."

"What's that got to do with him breaking into my house?" The smell of burning bacon filled the air. LeMar jumped up and went over to the stove to finish breakfast.

"You remember that card game we started?"

"Yeah, that illegal game that I warned you would get you into trouble."

Eddie slouched in his seat and ran his fingers across his forehead. "Yeah, well, I kept a book with all the players and figures in it. I thought if I ever wanted to start another game I could call on those guys again."

LeMar threw the eggs into the skillet and turned to Eddie. "You kept records on guys playing an illegal game? Don't tell me Dru's after you for that?"

"Not just that. From time to time he would sell them a little something. I kept up with who was purchasing what and how much. That's what he wants."

"Damn, Eddie, I can see why you keep getting yourself into so much trouble. You do some of the dumbest stuff."

Eddie didn't respond. He looked up when he heard the floor above them squeak. He smiled at LeMar. "Got company?"

LeMar kept cooking and pulled out two plates. "Yeah. So, why don't you just give Dru the book?"

"I can't." Eddie stopped tapping his fingers against the table and looked at LeMar. "Who's upstairs?"

"None of your business, man." LeMar pulled a tray down from the cabinet. He put Rosie's plate and a cup of coffee for her on the tray. He turned to Eddie. "Are you finished?"

Eddie stood up, laughing. "I know Rosie's not up there, is she?"

He gave LeMar an uneasy, puzzled look, but LeMar ignored him and walked out of the kitchen with the tray. Eddie followed. "I told you, it's none of your business. Thanks for the information, I'll be sure to let the police know."

LeMar walked toward the front door, but Eddie didn't. LeMar set the tray on the hall table and looked at Eddie. "If you don't mind, I've got company."

Eddie laughed out loud. "Man, oh, man. I don't believe this. It didn't take you long, did it? You found out she was divorced and jumped on that. Did she tell you why she got married in the first place?"

Rosie heard loud voices coming from downstairs and decided to go see what was going on. She grabbed her underwear from the foot of the bed and put it back on. Not wanting to slip back into her dress, she found LeMar's robe behind the door in the bathroom. After wiping her face, she stepped out of the bedroom and walked down the hall.

"Man, what are you talking about? I don't want to have this discussion with you. She can tell me whatever I need to know." He walked over to the front door. "Come on, I'll have to catch you later, my food's getting cold."

"Oh, so you know all about the baby. How she married that guy to give your baby a daddy."

LeMar shook his head and laughed. "Man, you'll try anything, won't you?"

When Eddie didn't say anything, but stared intensely at him, LeMar shook his head. "I didn't think so."

"Ask her." Eddie didn't move.

"I will. But I need for you to leave."

"Sure, I need to run up and get something—"

"Now, Eddie," LeMar insisted, holding the door open.

Eddie strolled over to the door, then stopped to look up the stairs first. Rosie stood there, looking down at him. He winked at her before walking out.

LeMar slammed the door behind him. He stood there for a few seconds before picking up the tray and turning toward the stairs. When he looked up, Rosie looked down at him, horror-struck.

Nineteen

Nausea welled in Rosie's stomach. She swallowed dryly. The look of uncertainty on LeMar's face made chills run down her spine. She backed up as he came up the stairs. When he reached the top, he looked at her. She trembled and opened her mouth to speak, but nothing came out.

He took the tray of food into the bedroom and set it down on the nightstand. "Here's your breakfast," he said, without looking back at her. He walked over to look out the window.

She stood in the doorway, cursing herself and wishing like hell she'd told him last night. She didn't want him to find out like this. But how did Eddie know?

"LeMar, I was going to tell you."

He dropped his head, then quickly spun around and gawked in disbelief. "No." He walked over to the bed and sat down. Leaning forward, he rested his forehead in the palms of his hands.

"I told you a lot happened after you left that—"

"A baby, Rosie. You didn't tell me about a baby." He held out his hands as if he were pleading to her.

"I didn't tell you I lost the baby—no." She walked into the room and sat on the opposite side of the bed. "Don't judge me until you know the whole story. I was pregnant, and you were gone."

He shot her a narrow-eyed look. "Don't do that. Don't you dare try to say I left you pregnant. You knew where I was."

"I didn't find out I was pregnant until two months after you were gone. By then, you had somebody else and had moved on with your life."

He jumped up. "I didn't have anybody else. Why is that so hard for you to believe?"

"Because you wouldn't talk to me. LeMar, you distanced yourself from me so fast. What was I supposed to think?"

He walked over to his dresser and slammed his fist on it. With his elbow resting on top, he pinched the bridge of his nose. "How could you do that to me? How could you not tell me you were pregnant with my child?" He slowly turned his head in her direction. "Help me understand that."

When she didn't answer, he walked back over to the bed and sat down. "Or was it my baby?" he asked coldly.

Now it was her turn to look shocked and horrified. "What do you mean, was it your baby? Who was I with every day of the week? Who had I made a commitment to? Who upset me so bad I dropped out of school and withdrew for weeks? You know it was your baby," she bellowed ferociously.

Enraged, she got up from the bed and walked over to the tray. She grabbed a piece of bacon and bit into it. Her appetite was gone.

"If you were so freakin' upset over me, how the hell could you turn around and marry the next man that came along? And did he know you were pregnant with *my* child?"

She turned around to find his grim face. His

mouth had tightened into a stubborn line. She could see the muscles twitching in his jaw. His voice was cold as ice. She'd never seen LeMar this upset before.

She leaned back against the table. "Yes, he knew I was pregnant. I didn't want to have—"

"But did he know it was *my* baby?" he asked bitterly.

She didn't like what he was accusing her of. She threw the rest of the bacon on the plate and stormed over to pick up her dress. How could he think such a thing about her?

She threw the dress over her shoulder and started removing his robe. Tears welled in her eyes.

LeMar stepped over, pulled the dress from her shoulder, and threw it on the bed. She tried to reach out and catch it, but he grabbed her wrist. She tried to jerk away as he pulled her to face him. Tears were streaming down her cheeks now.

"Okay, okay. Look, I'm sorry." He held her wrist out to the side. "This is just . . . you should have told me." He lowered her hands and gently let go.

He backed up and sat down. "Keep talking. I want to know why you married this guy."

"So I wouldn't have a baby out of wedlock. He offered to marry me so my baby would have a last name. David was a good friend, that's all." She slumped down into the bedroom chair. Her throat was dry, and she was completely exhausted.

"All you had to do was tell me. Your baby had a last name—Reed."

"How, when I couldn't reach you? I had people telling me you'd started dating someone else. The one time we did talk right before I lost the baby you admitted to going out with someone else."

He shook his head. "Rosie, I told you I went to a movie with somebody, not that I was involved, or even

serious with anybody. I was trying to see where your
head was. I didn't know you'd cut me off and tell
your family not to let me talk to you. I was coming
back at some point, and we could have stayed together."

"At some point! When was that going to be?"

"Apparently, not soon enough. But if I had known
about the baby, it would have been sooner. Don't you
know I would have left D.C. and come back to Atlanta?"

"Really?" She crossed her arms.

"Yes," he said with strong conviction.

Her eyes traveled from his head to his feet. He sat
on the bed in nothing but his boxers, stripped almost
naked with a desperate look in his eyes. She believed
him. She had to believe him.

"The night I left, I told you that wasn't the end
of us. It didn't have to be." He shook his head.

"You didn't say you weren't coming back, either. A
two-week trip turned into twelve years."

He looked up at her and they stared at each other
in silence. He finally looked away and got up. He
grabbed his pants from the foot of the bed and put
them on. She'd just made one of the biggest mistakes
of her life. He walked over to pick up the breakfast
tray.

"Last night never should have happened," she said,
hugging her legs.

He stopped in front of her, but she never looked
up at him. A few seconds later, he walked out.

"Okay, that's the second request for a consultation
this week. And both of them are a direct result of
the Colony House." Doreece spoke to Rosie from her
table, but Rosie seemed to be miles away.

"What's up with you? You haven't said two words this morning."

Rosie shook her head. "Nothing."

"Yeah, okay." Doreece walked over to the story-board for LeMar's house. She looked down at Rosie's notes. When she looked back at her sister, Rosie pretended to be writing something, but Doreece knew better.

"What happened?"

Rosie didn't respond.

"You hear me talking to you. What happened?"

Throwing her pen on the table, Rosie looked across the room at her sister. "Nothing. How many times do I have to tell you? Can't you see I'm trying to work?"

"Bull. You spent a night at his house, and haven't been right since then. What did he do to you?"

"It was a mistake. I should have carried my butt home, that's all."

"So what, the sex wasn't good?"

"I didn't say that."

"Then what the hell's going on? You haven't said two words to me all week. Those pictures came in that you ordered for his office, and they're still sitting in the boxes. I don't think you've worked on his house at all this week, have you? Or Neville, for that matter?"

"I've been busy. Could you take the pictures by there this afternoon? I'll give Neville a call and have him hang them for me. All I need you to do is drop them off."

"I'm not going to do your dirty work for you."

"Please, Doreece?"

Rosie had never begged her for anything. Doreece was puzzled by the desperate look on her face. Something had gone wrong. "Sure, I'll run them by."

* * *

LeMar burst into his office and closed the door behind him. He threw a folder onto his desk and his pen after it. There was a tap at his door.

"Yeah," he said in a huff.

The door slowly opened, and Grace poked her head in. "Hey, you okay?"

He pulled out his chair and sat down. He spun around and looked out the window. "I'm fine."

She continued into the office and closed the door behind her. "So what happened, did somebody steal your bike or something?"

Resting his elbows on the chair's armrests, he touched all his fingertips together and stared down at his hands. He knew he overreacted, but he couldn't help it. Everything was pissing him off. Even Grace.

"You've been in a funky mood all week. What gives?" She sat down in the chair across from his desk.

He slowly turned around, staring at her. Why was she in his office? "I've got a lot on my mind right now, if you don't mind."

She shrugged. "I just figured you could use somebody to talk to. You lashed out at those poor co-op students like they created our computer problems. They didn't; they're here to help."

He let out a loud sigh and dropped his hands in his lap. "It's going to take two weeks of overtime to get us back on track. I'm not happy about that."

"I know, but it's not the end of the world. That little Asian girl, Chris, walked out of that room with tears in her eyes."

"Grace, are you working on this project?"

"Yes, I am."

"Then I think you've got work to do," he said, coming to his feet.

She left his office.

Rosie picked up Carrie at six o'clock sharp for her weekly grocery visit. She dreaded it, knowing she'd ask about the party. They hadn't talked about it since that night.

"Did that young fella get those pictures developed yet? I want to see them."

"No, ma'am, not yet." Rosie had forgotten all about the photographer she'd hired for the event. She made a mental note to call him tomorrow.

"Well, you haven't told me, did you have a nice night? How was the party?"

She couldn't get to the grocery store fast enough. "It was very nice. You should have come."

"No, honey. You kids stay up too late for me. Did you enjoy yourself?"

Rosie knew what she really wanted to know. Doreece was right, Carrie was a nosy little lady. But she still loved her. "I had a great time. Everybody did."

"That's good. Did LeMar show up?"

Rosie glanced over at her. "You know darn well he showed up." She smiled at her.

"I wasn't too sure he'd make it. He said he wasn't sure himself."

"Yeah, well, he was there. And before you ask, he had a good time, too." She hoped she didn't ask anything else about him.

"He's such a nice young man, don't you think?"

"He's okay."

"I know you're not aware of this, but he told me about your past together."

"Well, that made you guys even, because you told him a little about my present situation—right?"

"I'm sorry, I wasn't aware that he didn't know."

"That's okay. He was going to find out sooner or later."

"Do you plan on seeing him again?"

"I guess so. I'll have to finish his house."

"I don't mean like that."

"That's the only way I plan on seeing him. You have to stop all this matchmaking. I'll find the right man for me."

"Honey, I think you've found him."

Rosie shook her head. "No, you don't understand. He's not the one."

"That's the fella you were dating in college before you met David, right?"

She shook her head. How had David entered this conversation?

"Then I think he is the one. You know, God works in mysterious ways. David told me about the baby."

Stunned, Rosie looked at her, shaking her head. "What did he tell you?"

"That he wasn't the father." She smiled sadly. "Rosie, David would have been there for you because he's a good man. He would have been a father to your baby, because he loves children. But I'm not sure that he would have been the right man."

"How come you never said anything?"

"He asked me not to ever mention it to you."

Rosie had always assumed their bond was based on the fact that Carrie thought Rosie had lost her great nephew. But now she knew better.

"I'm shocked, what can I say?"

"Does LeMar know about the baby?"

"He does now."

"Then it's not too late for you two."

Rosie laughed and stopped her. "Hold on. Just because we had something in the past doesn't mean we're meant to be or anything like that."

"I think you've been waiting for him."

"I've what?" She laughed as she pulled into the grocery store parking lot. "You've got to be kidding. I didn't even know he was coming back into town."

"I mean subconsciously. You always claim you're too busy to date."

"You and Doreece seem to have a handle on what my subconscious has been doing lately."

"Now, look at your little sister. She's going to be married with a family pretty soon. You need to listen to us."

Rosie killed the engine. "Mrs. Carrie, can we shop without bringing up LeMar? I don't want to think about him anymore this evening."

Carrie pulled a long piece of paper from her purse. "Honey, that's fine with me. I've got a lot of groceries to get, I'm expecting guests soon."

Doreece had the key Rosie'd given her and the pictures in the backseat of her car. When she pulled up to LeMar's house, his car was in the driveway. She wouldn't need the key after all.

This was the first time she'd ever been there alone. The house was truly beautiful. Her sister was good at her job. She was proud of her. She rang the doorbell and stood with the pictures leaning against her leg.

LeMar opened the door with raised brows. "Doreece, is something wrong?"

"No, everything's fine." She picked up the pictures. "Rosie asked me to drop these off."

"Come on in." He held the door open and took the pictures from her once she stepped inside.

"She said to leave them in the office, and Neville would know what to do with them tomorrow."

He set the pictures against the foyer wall. He tried to peek inside, but they were sealed shut. He turned back to Doreece. "Thanks, I guess she was too busy to bring them by herself?"

She shrugged. "Something like that." Her sister had put her in such an awkward position. She liked LeMar, and wanted him and Rosie to work out whatever had happened between them.

"It's just as well." He shrugged and gave her an it-really-doesn't-matter look.

"LeMar, I don't know what happened between you guys, but whatever, it's driving her crazy. She won't talk to me and she's grumpy."

He crossed his arms and slowly nodded his head, acknowledging he'd heard her, but he didn't respond.

"I'm not asking you what happened. I'm just trying to say I think it's a shame you guys can't work it out. I've seen the way you two look at each other."

His facial expression softened. "Thanks for your concern."

"Well." She turned to leave, but stopped and turned back. "You know, that day she ran into you at Mick's, I thought she was going to have a heart attack. She would never admit it, but I know she was excited to see you."

"I think she's gotten over that now."

"I don't know. Just don't give up on her. And don't hurt her again," she said with a twist of her lips.

"Doreece, I love your sister, and I'd never intentionally hurt her. If she'd only told me about the baby, none of this would have happened."

Doreece stood looking at him, stupefied. "Baby? What baby?"

Twenty

When Doreece walked back into the office, Rosie was on the phone. Doreece couldn't wait for her to get off so she could ask her about the baby. From the smile on Rosie's face, she knew the call was good news.

Rosie hung up and jumped from her seat. "Guess what?"

"You got another big job?"

"No. I made the cut."

"What cut?"

"*Design House* magazine. I've been selected as one of the top five interior designers of Atlanta."

Doreece applauded her. "I'm happy for you. Congratulations, sis."

"Thank you. Now all I have to do is talk LeMar into letting me use his house for the photo layout once it's finished. I think it'll look great in the magazine."

Doreece walked around to her table and sat down. She wasn't sure how to approach her sister with such a sensitive question.

"How did it go at LeMar's house with the paintings? Any trouble getting in?"

"No. I didn't have to worry about the alarm because he was there."

"He was?" Rosie asked.

"Yeah, and I want to know why you didn't tell me about the baby."

Rosie's jaw dropped. She couldn't believe her ears. "What did he tell you?"

"That you were pregnant with his baby, and you lost it. What I can't believe is that you never told me."

"He had no right to tell you that." She did want to tell Doreece, and she didn't want LeMar to do it for her.

"God, girl, I can't believe you were pregnant at any time, and I didn't know about it. How did you hide that?"

"I wasn't showing. I lost the baby after three months." Still in shock, Rosie placed her forehead in the palm of her hand. "I still can't believe he told you."

"He thought I knew. And now I'm thinking everybody knows except me. Do Mom and Dad know? How about Mrs. Carrie?"

"I told Mom when David and I got married. I never told Dad, so I don't know if he knows or not. And yes, Mrs. Carrie knows."

"Okay, some of this is making sense. I guess now I see why you didn't want to be around LeMar. But what did David have to do with it?"

Rosie exhaled. "It's a long story."

"That's okay." Doreece leaned back in her seat and crossed her arms. "I'm not going anywhere."

Rosie recalled everything from the moment she knew she was pregnant to her divorce from David. Some of the details Doreece already knew, but most she didn't.

Now everything was out in the open. She hoped

Doreece had a better understanding of why she had shielded her heart the way she had for so many years.

The week flew by for Rosie. She started another design job, but still hadn't returned to LeMar's house. Neville kept her informed of the progress. A couple of nights she'd wanted to pick up the phone and give Lemar a call, but always managed to decide against it.

She'd finally gotten back to her workout schedule. She turned the volume on the stereo up a few notches. She wanted to listen to her old Prince CDs while she rode her exercise bike. The music brought back wonderful happier memories. She was doing fine until "Let's Have a Baby" came on. All she could see was LeMar's face—him gawking at her in disbelief. Her pace slowed, but she kept going. Then she stopped when a verse from, "Nothing Compares 2 U" struck her. At that moment she knew Mrs. Carrie was right. No one had compared since him. She cut her workout short and jumped into the shower.

In the bathroom drying off, she heard a loud tapping noise. She threw on her robe, and went into the bedroom. Someone was at the door, banging like crazy.

Irritated, she ran downstairs and peeked out the door. *What?!* She opened the door.

"Surprise! You gonna let me in or what?"

Rosie stepped back, blinking. "I don't believe it."

"What, you didn't know I was coming?"

She tightened her robe and stood aside to let David in.

"Now I know Aunt Carrie told you I was coming."

He stopped on the way in and gave her a quick kiss on the cheek.

He'd always kissed her on the cheek. "Yes, she said you were coming, but she didn't say when. To what do I owe the honor?" She stood with her arms crossed and eyed him from head to toe. He looked good. He'd shaved his head and let his facial hair grow. He looked like a different man. His dimpled face was more masculine than when they were married.

"Now, come on, don't tell me I can't visit my ex-wife in our house." He walked into the living room, examining everything.

Rosie cleared her throat. "Ah, that would be my house now," she clarified.

He snapped his fingers. "Right. Sorry." He nodded and grinned as he surveyed the room. "I see you made some changes. It looks good."

She'd completely redecorated the place, but he'd never noticed any of her decorating anyway. "I did a little something. You know. Had to give it my touch."

He walked over to the couch. "Mind if I have a seat?"

"No, go ahead. How have you been?" she asked, sitting across from him.

"Great. Everything's going good. How about yourself?"

She smiled graciously. "I can't complain. I heard you opened your own business, too. How's that coming along?"

"It's been crazy, and exciting at the same time." He spent the next half hour telling Rosie all about his contract packaging business.

They had always been good friends. The marriage was what had messed up their friendship. Rosie was happy for David and his new business. However, she knew he wouldn't feel the same way about hers. As his friend, it would have been fine for her to have her own business, but not as his wife.

When he thought they would get married, have a baby, and she'd stay at home, he was fine. As soon as she lost the baby and wanted to work, David changed. He wanted her dependent upon him, and she couldn't do that. She wasn't that type of woman. Her mother had taught her to be independent.

After he told her all about his business, she squeezed in a little about hers. He appeared to listen more than in the past.

"You're really making a go of it, aren't you?" he asked, sounding surprised.

"I most certainly am. You should never have doubted me." She gave him a satisfied smile.

"Oh, I didn't doubt you. I knew it was going to be a lot of work. You know, most small businesses fail within the first few years, so I wish you luck."

"Thank you, and the same to you." She smiled thinly.

He leaned forward on the couch. "Hey, why don't you get dressed. I've got something I want to show you at Aunt Carrie's."

"What?" she asked, knowing he wasn't going to tell her. He loved surprises.

"Come on, get dressed, you'll see. It'll only take a few minutes."

She stood to leave the room. "Okay, I can only stay a minute. Hold on and let me throw on some jeans."

"I'm gonna grab a glass of water, if it's okay." He stood.

"Yeah, the glasses are in the same place. Help yourself." She ran upstairs.

* * *

After a week of walking around mad at the world, LeMar needed to talk to Rosie. He wanted to clear the air. He still loved her, no matter how upset he was.

He pulled up outside Rosie's house and sat there, staring out the window. He remembered what her sister had said when she'd come by. He had to at least try it again. "Here goes nothing," he said aloud. He got out, walked up to the front door, and rang the bell.

To his surprise, a man answered the door.

"Hello."

LeMar felt a sense of déjà vu. He wanted to know who this guy was. Possibly one of Rosie's clients, or a designer friend? "Hello, is Rosie home?"

"Yeah, she's here." He gestured vaguely toward the stairs after slightly looking up at LeMar. "She's upstairs getting dressed right now."

Getting dressed. LeMar wanted to get a good look at this guy. Maybe she was involved with him. If so, why had she slept with him?

"I'm a client of hers. I stopped by to speak to her for a moment if she's available."

He motioned LeMar in. "Come on in. I'll let her know you're here."

LéMar stepped inside the living room.

Rosie came down the stairs as David closed the door. "Who's at the door?"

LeMar turned and faced her. She stopped and looked from LeMar to David. Never in a million years had she thought this would ever happen. She told her feet to keep moving and slowly continued down the stairs.

"I'll be in the kitchen." David discreetly left the room.

Rosie made her way across the room with her eyes wide open in surprise. "'Hello. What's up?"

"Uh—it looks like Neville is finished with the house, so I wanted to stop by and thank you for a job well done." He gestured behind her. "I'm sorry, I didn't know you had company."

She looked back over her shoulder. "Let's step out on the porch."

He followed her. "I shouldn't be here. I'm not even sure why I came by." Stress lines formed across his brow. "I know my timing sucks." He tried to laugh, but wasn't very successful.

"It's okay. Did you have something you wanted to talk to me about?"

He hesitated for a moment, looking down at his shoes. "I actually stopped by because I felt uncomfortable about what went down last week. And I wanted to apologize. My response was insensitive, and I know it."

She shook her head. "I should have told you. It's my fault. I should have told Doreece, too."

"I wish you had. I had no idea that she didn't know." He looked up at the door, wanting to know who her company was. He knew full well he had no right to ask.

"Don't worry about it. I talked with her. We're cool. She forgives me for not telling her." She looked at him, wanting to know if he felt the same way.

He gazed at her, shaking his head. "You know, I'm gonna go. I just felt like I needed to see you." He started down the stairs.

"Thanks for stopping by. I appreciate it."

He glanced up at her. "You're welcome." He'd

wanted to talk to her about working things out, but all that had changed when he'd seen her company.

David returned to the living room when he heard the door close. Rosie stood inside the doorway, looking out.

"Is that your boyfriend?"

She spun around on him so quickly she made herself dizzy. "No, he's a client. David, what did you come by here for again?" She did not want him to know that was LeMar.

He clasped his hands together. "Come next door. I've got somebody I want you to meet."

"Who?" she asked. She held up her hand, letting him know she wasn't leaving until he told her.

"My fiancée."

Taken totally off guard, she put her hands on her hips, smiling. "Your what?"

He smiled back. "Yeah, I'm getting married." He rubbed his palms together.

"Congratulations. I mean it, I'm really happy for you."

"I know you are. Genuine friendship is something that we always had. That's why I want you to meet her. Come on, let's take a walk. She's next door, and I know Aunt Carrie is driving her crazy by now."

She eagerly grabbed her keys and went to meet his fiancée.

LeMar walked in from work Friday night tired and frustrated. Two of his contract employees had quit the same day. He'd spent most of the afternoon on the phone with human resources, trying to find replacements. Now someone was knocking at his door. He didn't feel like being bothered.

He opened the door to the same two police officers who worked his break-in. Maybe they'd found his stolen equipment since Eddie had given him a lead.

"Hello, Mr. Reed, we're looking for Eddie Spencer. Does he live here?"

"Not anymore, he moved out a few weeks ago. What's the problem?"

"We'd like to ask him a few questions. When's the last time you saw him?"

Eddie was in trouble. LeMar knew it. He'd hoped this wouldn't happen. "A couple of weeks ago. He dropped by for a few minutes." He explained how Eddie had given him the lead that he'd fed to the police about the break-in.

"Do you know where he lives now?"

He shook his head. "No idea." If they wanted to find him, let them do it the hard way. He wouldn't be the one to turn his buddy in. Besides, all he could do was get them in the area. Even he hadn't found out exactly where Eddie lived.

After the police left, LeMar changed clothes and ran out to his car. He rode around to some of the nightclubs and strip joints he knew Eddie frequented. There was no sign of him. He got back home around two o'clock in the morning.

Once he finally lay down, he felt the tension in his body. He couldn't relax. Something was wrong, he knew it. Eddie had gotten in over his head if the police were looking for him.

Just when Eddie appeared to be turning his life around with a job, now this. LeMar decided he'd go out to the airport the next day to see if he could find him. Considering the size of Hartsfield Airport, even finding anyone who knew Eddie was a long shot.

But he had to try. He had to warn Eddie the police were looking for him.

He didn't have a phone number, address, or anything. And though they'd been such good friends, he'd never met Eddie's girlfriend. He had no way of reaching his buddy.

The next morning, dressed and ready to drive out to the airport, LeMar opened his front door to see Rosie coming up the front steps.

"Hello. I've come to do the walk-through, remember?"

"Oh, yeah," he said hurriedly. "I forgot about that. This is Saturday morning, isn't it?"

"Is this a bad time? Were you on your way out?"

"I've got time, come on in." Eddie would have to wait.

She walked straight into the den, set her briefcase on the table, and opened it. She pulled out a long sheet of paper that detailed her work.

"Can I get you anything? Something to drink?" he offered.

"No, thank you. This won't take long. We can do a quick walk-through in no time."

"Sure, where do you want to start?"

"How about upstairs? Then we can work our way down."

"Cool." He led the way. He couldn't think of anything but asking Rosie who that guy was at her house. They walked through each room and surveyed the changes. She made sure they were to his satisfaction. When they entered one of the guest rooms, LeMar saw something on the floor that caught his attention. He reached down and picked up a small notebook of some sort lying just under the nightstand.

"What's that?" she asked.

He shrugged. "You think it might be something Neville lost?"

"I don't know." Now she shrugged.

He flipped the book open and noticed Eddie's handwriting. It looked like the book Eddie had mentioned. Possibly the same book Eddie claimed Dru was looking for? "This is Eddie's," he said, shoving the book into his pocket.

"Oh."

He furrowed his brow. "Come on, I'm sorry. Let's continue with the walk-through." If this was the book Eddie had tried to tell him about, he needed to find him. He didn't want anyone else getting hurt over that little book.

They finished the upstairs, then went downstairs to his new office area. He couldn't hold his thoughts any longer.

"Rosie, since you're here, I'd like to talk about what happened between us a couple of weeks ago." He sat on the edge of his desk. She looked up and sighed.

"I know you think it was a mistake. I want to know if you feeling that way has anything to do with that guy who was at your house."

She dropped her arms to her sides. "No, it had absolutely nothing to do with him."

"Can I ask who he was?"

She bit her bottom lip, looking at him as if she needed time to think about it. "David Wright."

His eyebrows shot up in surprise. "Your ex-husband?"

She nodded. "Yes."

Twenty-one

He nodded and scratched at the side of his head. "So, what's going on? Is he back in your life after all?"

"No. He was in town visiting Mrs. Carrie, that's all."

"Were you glad to see him?"

She let out a heavy sigh. "LeMar, David and I never should have gotten married, and we both recognize that. We'll remain friends, but that's it."

"What if he wants you back?"

"He doesn't. He brought his fiancée with him. He's getting married, and he wanted me to meet her."

Again, LeMar raised his brows in surprise. "He did?"

"Yes. Like I said, we're friends, and I wish him the best."

He looked into her eyes to see if he believed her, and he did. She'd always had a level head on her shoulders, and that was one of the things he loved about her. "I'm glad to hear that."

She held up her list. "Shouldn't we finish up?"

He got to his feet and walked over to her. Standing close enough to smell the flowery scent of her perfume, he resisted the urge to kiss her. Instead, he reached out for the list. "Let me take a look at that." He scanned it. "Everything's fine. Where do I sign it?" He looked down at her.

"I've got a pen in my purse." She took the list back and left the office.

He followed her into the den. They needed to talk. He wanted to set everything right between them. If she left his house without talking about it today, he might never get the opportunity again. However, he didn't know where to begin.

She laid the paper on the table and reached inside her purse for a pen.

The phone rang.

"I'm sorry, I can't seem to find a pen. Do you have one?" she asked.

LeMar stood to go answer the phone. "Uh, yeah. Check in the drawer over there. I'll be right back."

She walked over to the cabinet under the television and opened the drawer.

When he returned, she was standing with the drawer open, staring inside.

"Find a pen?" he asked.

"No. When did you start carrying a gun?" She pointed to the weapon in the drawer.

He walked over and shut the drawer. "It's not mine. It's Eddie's."

"I hope he hasn't gotten you involved in whatever he's into. LeMar, I'm telling you, he's going to get himself killed running around with those roughnecks. I've seen the guys he hangs out with, and their gangsters." She said all that at ninety miles per minute, without taking a breath.

"Hey, hey, relax. I'm not running with Eddie. I took the gun away from him so he wouldn't wind up getting himself killed. I forgot it was in there, that's all."

She walked over to the couch and sat down.

He could see the worry etched on her face. "It's nice to know that you care," he added.

She shrugged, averting her eyes and looking down at the contract. "I don't want to see anybody get hurt."

"Anybody or me?"

She looked up at him with pleading eyes. "You. I don't want to see *you* get hurt again."

He walked over, searched through another drawer, and pulled out a pen. He returned and signed the paper. "I don't want to get hurt again, either. By anyone."

She folded the piece of paper and put it back into her briefcase.

LeMar reached over and took her hand. "Especially by you."

Rosie looked into his eyes, then lowered her head. "I was going to tell you that morning. I thought about it before Eddie came by. For the life of me, I don't know how he knew." She looked back up at LeMar. "I think he's been hinting for weeks that he knew something about me."

"A couple of weeks ago we got into a fight, and he accused me of stealing you from him. He thinks you guys should have hooked up."

"When he saw that you stayed the night, I'm sure he was mad, and he wanted to hurt me."

She shook her head. "I was never remotely interested in him."

"I know. Do you think we can talk about the baby? I mean, I don't know what happened or anything. Was it a girl or a boy?"

"A boy. Everything was going fine, then one day I was at work, and my stomach started cramping. I called David, who came and took me to the hospital.

I told my coworkers I was sick. They didn't even know I was pregnant. We went to the emergency room, and at one-fifteen P.M. I lost the baby."

"Oh." Sadness enveloped LeMar as he laid his head back onto the couch. "Rosie, I'm really sorry."

She nodded, smiling at him. "Losing a child hurts like hell. But David was there, being a friend to help me get through it."

"I'm glad he was there for you, but that should have been me."

"Well, it's history now. I've gotten past it, and moved on with my life. One day, when it's meant to be, I'll have children." She picked up her briefcase. "I'm glad you like the house. The walk-through concludes the final phase. It was a pleasure." She reached out to shake his hand.

"I love the house, no question about that." He held on to her hand. "Does this mean I won't be seeing you again?"

"Maybe not, but I have a favor to ask of you."

"Shoot."

"I was chosen by *Design House* magazine as one of the top five designers in Atlanta, and they want to do a photo shoot of one of my projects. Quite naturally, I thought of your house. Would you mind?"

He clapped for her. "Bravo. That's wonderful. And you didn't even have to ask. I'd be honored."

"Thank you, LeMar."

"Is that the only time I'm going to see you?"

"LeMar, I haven't changed my mind. I think we may have had some unresolved feelings that we needed to get out once and for all that night. But I'm not sure it's wise for us to try and rekindle what we had." She let go of his hand and headed for the front door.

"I think you're wrong," he said, shaking his head.

"You said our making love was a mistake. Well, I think you're making the mistake now."

"If it was meant to be, it would have been. And I never would have lost the baby."

She said good-bye and left his house.

After Rosie left, LeMar headed for the airport, with the notebook in his back pocket. After two hours of talking to skycaps, ticket takers, counter sales staff, and even a few cleaning employees, he couldn't find anyone who knew Eddie. Realizing this was like looking for a needle in a haystack, he gave up and went home. He placed the notebook in the same drawer with Eddie's gun. When Eddie finally came around, LeMar would give them to him.

LeMar's secretary, Brenda, slipped into his ten o'clock meeting and passed him a note. He opened it and read that an Officer Williams wanted him to call as soon as possible. He hoped that meant they'd found his stolen goods.

After the meeting, he went back to his office. Brenda's desk was outside of his. He approached her desk first.

"So, Brenda, what did this Officer Williams say?"

"Nothing really. I told him you were in a meeting, and he said to have you call. He did say it was very important."

"I hope he's got my stuff. I had to buy a new computer, but I'd like to get my VCR and DVD player back."

"Look at it this way. If you don't get them back, you can take the insurance money and buy even better ones."

"Yeah, but I had nice ones." He looked down at the note. "Guess I'd better give him a call." He walked into his office and closed the door.

"Officer Williams please." It took more than five minutes for him to come to the phone. LeMar almost hung up.

"This is Officer Williams."

"Hello, it's LeMar Reed. My secretary said you called."

"Yes, Mr. Reed. I'm afraid we've got some bad news."

LeMar leaned back in his chair. It looked like the police were giving up, and he'd have to go shopping for new electronics.

"You're closing my case?" he speculated.

"Sir?"

"My electronics, you've given up on finding them?"

"No, sir. What I'm calling for is to inform you that your friend Eddie Spencer was shot last night in front of the Gentlemen's Club."

LeMar bolted out of his seat. "You're kidding."

"I'm afraid not, sir."

"Is he okay?"

"No. He was pronounced dead on arrival at Grady Hospital."

The news hit him like a sledgehammer. His stomach contracted into a knot of grief. Leaning forward, he held the phone with one hand and placed his head in the palm of his other hand. "Damn, Eddie."

"Mr. Reed, my partner and I were at your house a couple of days ago looking for him. We wanted to question him about his involvement with a man named Dru Stone. Do you know him?"

LeMar rubbed his eyes, exhaling. He hardly heard a word the policeman said for thinking about Fast Eddie. "Dru, yeah, I've met him, but I don't know him. Eddie told me he might be responsible for my break-in. I called down to the police station and gave them his name."

"You did? When?"

He gave a frustrated sigh and leaned back in his seat again. "A couple of days ago. I called the police station, gave them my case number, and the name of a suspect—Dru Stone. I bet nobody looked into it, and now my friend's dead." He wanted to throw the phone across the room.

"I'll pull your case and look into it. In the meantime, do you know how we can reach his family?"

"I think I've got his father's phone number at home somewhere. I'll have a look and—" He suddenly remembered the little notebook.

"Mr. Reed, you still there?"

"Yes. I just thought of something. I found something the other day that I'd like to show you. It might help to find out who shot my friend."

"What is it?"

"A notebook my friend kept with information about an illegal card game. It's the book I think the burglars were looking for."

"How soon can you get here?"

"I'm leaving work now."

LeMar told Brenda he had to leave for the day, but he didn't tell her why. He didn't tell anyone. He ran home to get the notebook, then ran it over to the police station.

"Don't you want to know my good news?" Doreece pouted.

"Oh, I'm sorry. What's your good news?" Rosie had spent the last twenty minutes telling Doreece all about her new design job. It was a small bed-and-breakfast in historical Roswell, Georgia.

"It's going to be a boy." Doreece reached in her purse for the ultrasound picture.

"What?! I thought you guys were going to wait and be surprised."

"I tried, but I couldn't. When we went to have the ultrasound, Tony said, go for it." Doreece pulled the picture from her purse.

Rosie got up and walked over to see the picture.

"Don't be mad. Tony wanted to go with me. I didn't want to tell you in case he changed his mind. But he didn't." She held out the picture.

Rosie held the picture, tracing the figure of the baby with her finger. "There he is." Looking at that picture made her heart ache with sorrow. Maybe she hadn't actually gotten over losing her baby after all. Maybe she'd never get over it. She gave the picture back.

Doreece took the picture and reached over to hug Rosie. They embraced as Rosie blinked to hold back the tears. This was her sister's moment, and she didn't want to spoil it. "He's going to be a beautiful baby," she whispered.

"I'm going to frame it." Doreece sat back down and positioned the picture on her desk.

Rosie walked back over to her desk. "I would, too."

"That's not all my good news."

"No. What now?"

"He asked me to move in with him."

"To live with him?" she asked in alarm.

"Yes, but only until we get married, which we plan on doing next year, after the baby's born." Doreece announced.

Rosie nodded and smiled. "It would have been nice to do it before the baby arrives, but at least you guys are getting married. He sure changed his tune mighty fast."

"I told you he wasn't a bad guy."

"Yeah, I guess he's okay." She smiled.

The phone rang. Rosie looked at the clock. It was almost lunchtime. Before she picked up the phone, she called over to Doreece, "Hey, after this call, let's run and grab some lunch."

"Cool."

"Hello, Yahimba Designs."

"Rosie, are you sitting down?"

It was Sharon. She sounded nervous. "Yes, I am. What's wrong?"

"You remember my buddy Alex? He's a Fulton County cop?"

"Yeah, what about him?"

"He called me this morning. Guess what happened?"

"What, girl?"

"Eddie got shot last night."

"See, I knew something bad was going to happen to that little fool. How is he?"

"Rosie. He's dead."

She flinched and fell back in her seat. "Oh, my God. You're kidding."

"No, I'm not. Shot to death outside a strip club. I bet it was those guys he was running around with the night we saw him."

Doreece got up and walked over to Rosie's desk with raised brows. "What is it? What happened?"

She shook her head and kept talking to Sharon. "I told LeMar Eddie was going to get himself killed. Girl, that fast life wasn't for him. I hope LeMar didn't get mixed up in any of his mess." As she spoke, she remembered the gun she found, and LeMar saying it was Eddie's.

"Sharon, I'd better call LeMar. Eddie was his best friend. I wonder if he knows."

"Okay. Give him a call and call me back."

When she hung up, Doreece was right there. Rosie filled her in as she picked up the phone and dialed LeMar's office. His secretary answered.

"Hello, Brenda, may I speak with LeMar? It's Rosie Wright."

"I'm sorry, he's not available at the moment."

"If he's in a meeting, can you get him? It's urgent."

"Actually, he's not here. He ran out of here like a bat out of hell after the police called."

"What, the police?" Rosie hung up, praying LeMar had no involvement in whatever had happened.

Twenty-two

After he left the police station, LeMar rode around for a while. He went past the Gentleman's Club. Why couldn't Eddie have been there the night LeMar had been looking for him? Maybe he'd still be alive.

Then again, if he hadn't taken Eddie's gun and given it to the police, Eddie could have defended himself. LeMar didn't think it was registered. The police would probably find out that it was a stolen weapon.

After spending all evening at the police station, he didn't want to talk to anyone. When he got home, he had two frantic phone messages from Rosie. She wanted him to call her the moment he walked into the house.

He took off his clothes and climbed into the shower. Afterward, he fell across the bed and lay staring up at the ceiling. He'd tried to help Eddie, but had he tried hard enough? He should have gotten him a job. He should have insisted that he work in order to stay with him. Should have, could have, would have . . . it was too late now. He felt sorry for his little buddy. A tear rolled down the side of his face as he shut his eyes.

About an hour later, the phone woke him from a deep sleep. He rolled over and grabbed the receiver.

"Hello," he answered in a groggy voice.

"LeMar. Why haven't you returned any of my calls? Are you all right?"

Hearing Rosie's voice, he sat up on his elbow. "I'm fine. I'm just tired, that's all. You heard about Eddie?"

"Yes, Sharon told me. I'm really sorry. I know he was your friend and all."

"Thanks."

"So, who shot him? Do the police know?"

"Not yet. He got into an argument with some guy, they said. The guy pulled out a gun and shot him in the chest. He died in the ambulance on the way to the hospital."

"Poor thing."

"Yeah."

"Well, are you going to ask the police to watch your house or anything?"

"For what?"

"Whoever killed Eddie might come searching your house again."

"I don't think so. I gave the police a pretty good lead to the guys Eddie was hanging with. Plus, there were a few people across the street from the club who saw the whole thing."

"And they're talking to the police?"

"Yeah. They're from Memphis. They were in the hotel parking lot when the fight started."

"That's good, maybe they can identify the guy."

"Let's hope so."

The line fell silent. LeMar wanted to ask Rosie to come over. To be with him for a little while, but he didn't know what she'd say. She'd made it pretty clear that she didn't want to be with him.

"You know what I hate?" He broke the silence.

"What's that?"

"The last conversation I had with him was a fight. I kicked him out of my house. He acted like he wanted to go upstairs for something, but I wouldn't let him. He was probably going to get that little book."

"LeMar, don't blame yourself. Eddie got mixed up with whomever all by himself."

"I know that, but I can't help it." He hurt like hell, and he needed her right now.

"Well, I wanted to make sure you were okay, and to let you know I'm sorry."

"Rosie?"

"Yeah."

"Will you come over? I mean, right now? At this very moment, can you come over here?"

She sighed into the phone. "LeMar, I don't know."

"I need you."

The line fell silent again. He hoped she was thinking about it.

A few seconds later she said, "Give me about thirty minutes, I'll be there."

"Thank you."

Rosie got out of the car and hurried up the steps. Before she reached the front porch, the door swung open and LeMar stood there with a pained expression on his face. She wanted to reach out and hug him. She continued up the steps and into the house.

"Thank you for coming," he said as he closed the door behind her.

"No problem. Are you okay?"

He nodded. "Yes and no." He tilted his head. "I need some coffee. You want a cup?" He turned and started down the hall.

"No, I'm fine." She followed him.

In the kitchen he went to start the coffeemaker while Rosie took a seat. She didn't know what to say to him. How could she help? She hoped her presence was enough. He probably just didn't want to be alone.

"You know, he really wasn't a bad guy. He just wanted to be a little bigger than he was." He turned around to face her and leaned against the counter.

"Eddie was trying to compensate for so many things. When we were in school, and he didn't have any money, he wouldn't tell me. He'd just say he didn't feel like going out, or he wasn't hungry."

"Why didn't he call home for money like everybody else?" she asked.

LeMar pushed his hands behind him against the counter and looked down. "There wasn't anybody at home he could call. His mother was dead, and his dad kicked him out. He was doing it all on his own."

"How?"

He shrugged. "He had a grant and a job. But he kept losing his jobs. Then he got kicked out of school because his grades were so bad. He really was trying, though."

"Too bad he couldn't have held on to the jobs."

"He never could hold a job. I think he had too much on his mind. When he was eighteen and nineteen, he had to worry about where he was going to live and what he was going to eat. Not what classes he was going to take."

"Is that why you looked after him so much? You felt sorry for him?"

He looked up and fixed his coffee. "I didn't feel sorry for him. He had it in him to do the right thing; he just got tired of trying, so he started looking for shortcuts. I told him there were no shortcuts in life."

"Well, you did finally get through to him. You said

he got a job and moved into his own place." She tried to make him feel better. Although she didn't like Eddie, she didn't want to see him dead.

LeMar shook his head. "He didn't have a job. I told the police and they checked out the airport. There's no record of Eddie Spencer working anywhere out there. He probably didn't have an apartment, either." He walked over and sat down at the table.

"LeMar, stop beating yourself up. I'm sorry he's gone, but you tried to help him so many times."

He slouched down in his seat and leaned his head back against the high-back chair. He closed his eyes and let out a long sigh. "I know it's not my fault. I just think I could have prevented it."

"You can't prevent everything. Sometimes things happen for a reason. Maybe it was Eddie's time to go. Then it wouldn't have mattered what you did. We don't know what God has in store for us."

He looked up. "Do you think God gives us second chances?"

She swallowed. He looked at her with such intensity. "Sometimes, yes."

"Then what do you think this is? You and me being reunited like this after twelve years. You don't think it's a second chance?"

She shrugged, speechless.

"I tried to help Eddie back when we were in school. That was my first chance, but I didn't recognize it. I think this was my second chance to help, and I blew it. But you and I . . . I don't intend to blow this one."

Butterflies circled in her stomach as she looked away from him. Could he be right? Could everybody be right? She knew she still loved him.

He leaned forward, stretching his arm across the

table to touch her hand. "Rosie, when I made love to you, it was no mistake. I'd hoped it was the beginning of something. And I thought I sensed that from you, too."

She took a deep breath and looked down at his hand massaging hers. "LeMar, what about the baby and—"

"We can have another baby."

She looked up in surprise.

"I don't think God would have given us a second chance if we weren't meant to be. I want a second chance. What about you?"

She looked into his eyes, searching for an answer. "LeMar, I still hurt."

"So do I. But we can help each other through it. Let's erase the whole thing and start all over again." He looked into her eyes, pleading.

She was so nervous she felt herself start to shake. "Let me think about it." She pulled back her hand.

"Okay. I guess that's all I can ask for at this point."

"Well, it's getting late, and I've got an early appointment. Are you going to be okay?"

"I will be. Thanks for coming by."

They walked to the front door. He reached around and opened the door for her, then quickly shut it again.

She jumped with a start and looked up at him. "What's wrong?"

"I really want you to think about it. I feel as if I've been waiting for you for more than twelve years. There hasn't been anyone in my life that could touch the place you hold in my heart. I just want you to know that."

She wanted to cry. Was she insane for leaving this man right now? Was he her soul mate? She'd spent so many years never wanting or expecting to see him again. She needed to think.

"I'll call you." That was all she could say before running down the steps to her car.

Two days passed, and LeMar had spoken with Eddie's sister, who was making all his arrangements. He'd even finally met the infamous Kim, who he found out was a shake dancer at the Gentlemen's Club. He'd alerted Brenda that if Rosie called, he was to be disturbed from any meeting. But she hadn't called yet.

He was going crazy. He'd left his heart wide open to be crushed again. She knew exactly how he felt about her. What he needed to hear was whether she wanted him back.

The phone rang, and he looked at the caller ID. It wasn't Rosie's number. He started not to answer it, but decided she might be calling from another phone.

"Hello, LeMar Reed speaking."

"Mr. Reed. This is Officer Williams."

"Hello, officer, what can I do for you?"

"I've got some good news for you. We've recovered a few of your stolen items."

"You found them?"

"Yes, sir, we also found your friend's killer."

LeMar leaned way back in his seat and took a deep breath. It was over. "Who was it?"

"We've got a Dru Stone in custody. He had some of your friend's possessions on him at the time of the arrest. He later confessed."

LeMar pinched the bridge of his nose and thanked God.

***

Rosie sat at her desk, staring at the phone. She wanted to pick it up, but she was afraid. Could her heart take it if he hurt her again? Could she live another twelve years denying herself love because nobody lived up to him? She looked across the room at Doreece, who hummed happily to the radio while working.

"Doreece, do you think it's healthy to relive the past?"

She looked up and shrugged. "I guess. Why else would they call old songs oldies but goodies? And why do we always want to go back and be kids again?" She chewed on the end of her ink pen. "And if we didn't relive the past, we wouldn't have any fond memories."

Rosie chuckled, shaking her head. "That's good enough. Man, I better watch what I ask you. Being pregnant has made you more philosophical."

They shared another laugh, then the door opened. Rosie's face froze when LeMar stepped through the door. A surge of elation ran through her as her face flushed with happiness. He walked in, closing the door and glancing around the small office.

"Good afternoon, Doreece, Rosie." He politely spoke to the ladies.

"Hey, LeMar. It's good to see you. What brings you in?" Doreece asked, looking from him to Rosie. When he didn't answer, but only stared at her sister, she took the cue.

"I'm gonna run out and grab some lunch. Rosie, do you want me to bring you anything?"

Rosie shook her head and went to stand as LeMar walked over to her desk.

"Okay, I'll be back—tomorrow." Doreece slipped out of the office.

"Don't stand up." LeMar held out his hand. "You know, you always do that when I walk into the room."

She couldn't hold back the broad grin that engulfed her face. Nor could she stop the hot flash that consumed her body. He walked all the way over to her desk and sat on the corner.

She spun in her chair to face him. "Didn't I say I'd call you?"

"Yeah, yeah." He nodded with pouted lips. "But it's been two days, so I figured none of your phones were working. Because mine are working fine, they're just not ringing. Got any idea why?"

She bit her lip. "Why don't you try that phone over there." She pointed to the phone on Doreece's table.

LeMar looked at the phone, then back at Rosie. He stood and walked over to sit in Doreece's chair. Rosie picked up her phone and dialed her second line.

He smiled when the phone rang. Then he answered. "Hello, LeMar Reed speaking."

"Hello, Mr. Reed, this is Rosie Wright."

"Well, Mrs. Wright. I've been waiting for your call. I hope you have some good news for me."

"Actually, I have some very good news for you."

"And what would that be?" he asked, not talking into the phone. He looked across the room at her.

"I'm available this Friday night if you'd like to pick a girl up and take her on a date."

He hung up the phone and stepped back over to her desk. She stood.

"And I know the perfect place to take a girl." He moved closer.

"Where?" she asked, crossing her arms.

"There's this spot over on Ponce de Leon that I think you'll love." He grinned and stepped between

her and the desk, then planted a kiss on her forehead.

"How do you know I'll like it?" she asked in a coy
way.

"Because the decor is out of sight. And the host,
he'll make you feel like a queen. That is, if you'll
give him a chance."

"I've waited twelve long years to give him a second
chance." She stepped closer until one of her legs was
between his. He eased his arms around her waist.
"Besides, if we didn't relive the past, we wouldn't
have any fond memories."

LeMar held his head back. "What?"

She laughed. "Never mind. Kiss me."

Dear Reader,

I hope you enjoyed REUNITED. Rosie and LeMar lived with me for some years before they finally saw the light of day.

In case you were wondering, the name Yahimba is pronounced yah-HIM-bah, and it's from the African people of Nigeria, meaning "there is nothing like home."

I love to hear from readers, so if you'd like to drop me a line, please do so. Include a self-addressed, stamped envelope for a speedy reply. I can be reached at P.O. Box 76432, Atlanta, GA 30358.

Thank you,
Bridget Anderson